THE SECRET RIVER

It was gold that had brought Judy's father to Alaska, and the mine he was opening showed real promise. But, as young Rod Baird told Judy the first day she visited his store in Rampart Bay, the real gold of Alaska was not metal but salmon— the big king salmon and, more important, the 'pinks' that returned each year to spawn in the rivers. To own a trap on one of these rivers meant a good living, and there was keen competition for sites and tremendous expense involved in building the intricate traps.

Rod's scheme to rejuvenate the nearby Tallac River, which had once been the Indians' richest fishing ground, was dismissed as ridiculous by everyone except Judy, and of course Rod's own family, who spent all they had to prove him right. Judy was a little dismayed to find that her father sided with the powerful cannery owners, but nothing could shake her faith in Rod, for in her heart she knew that her future lay with him and with Alaska.

Readers of *Hidden Harbour* and *Second Meeting* will be happy to find the other members of the Baird family in this delightful new story, and all newcomers to Kathrene Pinkerton's novels will discover for perhaps the first time the beauty and excitement of life in Alaska.

THE
SECRET
RIVER

Kathrene Pinkerton

THE BODLEY HEAD
LONDON

© Kathrene Pinkerton 1958
Printed in Great Britain for
THE BODLEY HEAD LTD
10 Earlham Street, London WC2
by W. & J. Mackay & Co Ltd of Chatham
Set in Monotype Garamond
First published in Great Britain 1958

1

As the *Queen* nosed in to the Juneau wharf, Judy Randolph stood at the rail trying to find her father among the people who had come to meet the steamship from 'state-side.' She wasn't at all sure he'd be among them or even if he had received her cable saying she was sailing for Alaska. It was quite possible he hadn't, since the new gold mine at Shaman Cove was a day's travel down the coast. If her father was not in Juneau, she would have to find means of getting to him. She knew there must be some way to do it, and had considered asking Captain Jarvis of the *Queen*, then decided not to. She didn't want to explain that she'd left school in Boston, crossed the continent, and come to Alaska wholly on a sudden impulse. The captain, who had a daughter just her age, seventeen, had taken a special interest in her and her first voyage to Alaska, and undoubtedly would consider such behaviour startling. On the whole, it had seemed wiser to say nothing that would disturb his natural conclusion that she was expected by a father who had planned to have his daughter spend her vacation with him. She had hoped the idea would appear as logical to her father.

But now, with their meeting possibly only a few moments away, she wasn't nearly as certain as she had been when she'd left Boston. The explanation of why she had suddenly abandoned her plans for the summer and set off for Alaska practically overnight would be difficult, and, as the *Queen* crept closer to the wharf, she had a moment of swift panic. Then, as the lines were made fast and the gangplank was lowered, Judy saw her father step out from the group of people on the pier. She leaned over the rail to wave, and David Randolph lifted his hat and smiled.

She had determined to go to Alaska that June evening when all the things he had told her in his letters of the past few months had suddenly pieced together. First there had been the closing of the Lady Luck, his own gold mine in the

5

Mother Lode of California, then his delight, almost relief, when Marcia Fellows invited her to spend the summer at Bar Harbour after their graduation from Miss Leighton's. Her father ordinarily left vacation plans to Judy and her Aunt Nina, as being wholly women's problems, but this time he had written that he was increasing her allowance to make sure she had the proper clothes. The larger budget was far more than she needed, but she'd been touched by his evident desire to make up for not seeing her this summer, since he would be in Alaska exploring a new mine site for the Northwest Mining Corporation. As a geologist and engineer whose opinion was respected in the mining world, he was often away in distant places. Usually he arranged to visit in the East during her vacations or asked her to join him. He hadn't done so this year, and Judy thought this might be the reason for his concern about her summer. At least she'd thought so until his cheque arrived, only half of what he'd said it would be. But his letter told her not to scrimp because the summer after graduation was important. The rest of the money, he wrote, would reach her in July or early August.

The cheque had told her more than he'd ever be willing to admit. The closing of the Lady Luck must have been more disastrous than she had realized. She studied the cheque for a long time, imagining his troubled thoughts when he had sent it and knowing the sacrifice he must be making to give her a carefree summer in Bar Harbour.

The next day she cabled that she would meet him in Juneau and departed for Seattle before his reply could reach her. She packed her diploma as proof she was educated. Or perhaps 'finished' was the better word, she thought a bit ironically; ten years of boarding schools and two trips to Europe.

And now her father was waiting for her at the foot of the gangplank and looking as though he was really glad to see her. She was sure of this when he kissed her, but his greeting was as carefully casual as though a daughter dropping in for a visit in Alaska was an everyday affair.

'Hear you had a rough trip,' he said. 'But you look as though you had enjoyed it.'

6

'I did, Dad.' Judy laughed in sudden relief, then thought she should have known he'd be willing to wait to hear her story. 'It wasn't really rough,' she went on quickly, 'except for a few hours. Mostly rain and fog. I've hardly seen the shore since we crossed the boundary. Poor Captain Jarvis! With all those tourists who'd expected days of wonderful scenery! At least we had a grand morning to see Juneau. Isn't that mountain gorgeous! I couldn't quite believe it.' She looked at the snowy peak with the little town nestling at its feet. 'It's—it's like stage scenery.'

He smiled. 'At first sight it does seem so, but I'm sorry you missed seeing the Inside Passage because of fog.'

'That only made this morning more exciting. To wake up and find yourself in a world of sunlight, and such a—' She stopped as a steward came up with her luggage. Her father was staring at the number of bags with obvious astonishment. 'The travel agency warned me to bring warm clothing,' she explained quickly, 'and with summer things it made so much.'

'Don't worry. The three of us can manage. Alec's around here somewhere.'

'Alec!' she said. 'Did he come to meet me too! But I should have known he would.' Alec Russell had been her father's foreman for years, and now he stepped from the group of onlookers.

He grinned a welcome as he shook hands. 'You've changed a bit since I last saw you.'

'You haven't, Alec. You don't look a bit different from that first summer in Grass Valley when you took me horseback riding in the Sierras. Didn't we have fun?'

'Sure did, Judy,' Alec said, and looked at the array of bags. 'You used to travel lighter in them days. Never mind, we'll have your gear aboard in no time. You folks ready to pull out?'

David Randolph nodded. 'We'll have to, Judy, if we want to get in before dark. Shaman Cove is a good run from here.'

'I know,' she said. 'Captain Jarvis showed me on the chart.'

Alec started under a load of bags, and she and her father

7

fell behind him. 'I didn't know whether you would get my cable,' Judy said.

David Randolph looked at her sharply. 'Then you knew there was a chance I wouldn't?' he asked. 'It was sheer luck. Alec happened to come to Juneau for a shipment of machinery. By that time you had already sailed. Did your Aunt Nina know about your coming?'

'Of course. I told her we had—or maybe I had—changed our plans.'

'She must have been astounded! Only last month I had a letter telling me how happy she was that you were staying with the Fellows in Bar Harbour and how much such a summer could mean to you, this year especially.'

That, Judy thought, was why he had been so concerned and so unwilling to deprive her of it no matter what sacrifice it meant on his part. Her father and his only sister, Nina, hadn't always agreed on her education in the ten years since her mother's death, but in the main he had deferred to his sister's judgement. Judy was fond of her aunt, admired her enormously, and her house had been a second home. But for once Judy was certain Aunt Nina had been wrong, especially if she'd known about the Lady Luck. A summer in Bar Harbour wasn't that vital, not if it meant financial hardship for her father. But she couldn't tell him this now, at least not until she knew more about it. Besides, this wasn't anything you could leap off a steamship and say in your first half-hour. It would make him feel just awful.

'Aunt Nina understood I wanted a visit with you. We haven't seen each other since last August. I got the idea quite suddenly one evening. And so I came.' It wasn't the entire truth, and she suspected her father knew this, but he looked pleased despite it.

'And Nina approved?' he asked.

Judy laughed in some embarrassment. 'I'm sorry, but I didn't actually talk to her about it. She'd gone to New York on that fling she always takes before she opens the place at Martha's Vineyard, and so I had to write it in a letter.'

'Mailed, no doubt, on the eve of your departure,' he said dryly.

'Something like that,' she admitted. 'But I was coming anyway. Aren't you glad to see me?'

'I am, Judy. And we can talk about this later.'

They had turned off the wharf toward a float, where a line of gas boats was moored. Alec was already loading the bags aboard a boat. The grey paint on its wheelhouse was rust-stained, and it had evidently been built for heavy duty, but it had a small cabin amidships.

'Nothing fancy,' her father said. 'All we needed this summer was a craft to get around in.'

Judy laughed when she saw the name crudely lettered on the stern. ' "*Working Stiff*"!' she exclaimed. 'Did you name her, Dad?'

'Alec did. Her previous owner called her *Floradora Girl*, but an old hardrock man like Alec didn't consider it fitting for a gold mine.'

'It's a he, not a she,' Alec said. 'Got him entered on the payroll as a member of the crew. Come aboard and we'll get going.'

As they went out into Gastineau Channel, Judy looked back at the town. Its white buildings, sparkling in the sunshine, were in lovely contrast with the green slopes of the two mountains that towered above.

'See the chute on that nearer mountain?' her father said.

She nodded. She'd been wondering about it.

'That's a gold mine. Low grade ore, but they can make money because it's all downhill instead of expensive lifting in a shaft. And right beneath us is one of the finest gold mines in Alaska, the Treadwell. They've tunnelled out beneath the sea from Douglas Island across the channel.'

She blinked. One gold mine in a mountain, another beneath the sea. 'It's so different from the Mother Lode in California,' she said. 'And so much more exciting.'

'Sure,' Alec said. 'There're spots along here where you can see the peaks on the mainland. Big fellows. Six and seven thousand feet, and stacked in close, one right behind the other. Keep your eyes peeled when we get to Stephen's Passage for your first sight of an iceberg.'

'Icebergs!'

9

'They look mighty pretty riding out on the tide from Taku Glacier. Too bad, Boss, we ain't got time to run up to Taku and show her fresh ones just breaking off. Big as office buildings, and every shade of blue and green you can think of. But we'll do it some day, Judy. Can you take the wheel, Boss, while I stow the afterdeck?'

David Randolph grinned at Judy. 'This is to impress you,' he said. 'Alec doesn't usually trust me with the *Working Stiff*.'

'Rather do it now than later when we hit the strait,' Alec said. 'Might get shook up some out there, and I want to get this freight lashed down.'

Judy watched him as he walked aft. She couldn't imagine what her father would do without him. He'd been with David Randolph so many years and in so many places. 'But where did he learn about boats?' she asked.

'He was fussing around San Francisco Bay long before he came with me. And he can turn his hand to anything. Never been stumped in his life. I sent him to Alaska a month ahead, and when I arrived, the camp was ready. Shacks built, crew hired, a good cook installed, boat built, machinery unloaded.'

Judy stood in the wheelhouse door, thinking how close were these two, who had done so much together. Probably no two men had ever understood each other better. Suddenly she went to the afterdeck where Alec was working.

'Tell me,' she said quickly. 'Is the Lady Luck shut down forever?'

'Hasn't he told you?'

'Not yet.'

Alec shrugged. 'Wait until he does.'

'But I'm afraid he won't tell me. Not the whole truth. And—and I've got to know, Alec.'

Alec finished drawing a rope tight.

'Take it easy, Judy. Your father has been hit hard, two ways. Give him time. No man wants to talk about a thing like that.'

'But I've got to know, Alec.' She hesitated. 'Before we— talk about—about my coming up here. Don't you see?' Her voice was pleading.

Alec studied her for a moment.

'You know how he always was about mining,' he began. 'Ever since he left college. Never risked a nickel. Always on a salary. And that got big, he was so good. One of the best mining engineers in the business. Then this glory hole in the Mother Lode, the Lady Luck. Always before he'd been making millions for other people—being sure, and being right. And why couldn't he do the same for himself. He felt he was right and sure this time—the way he had always been before.' Alec threw a lashing across a box and pulled the knot tight with a vicious tug, than faced her. 'And the only time he ever took a chance, all his know-how had to go back on him. He sunk his savings into it, and that was plenty. Maybe borrowed besides. Now he's back on salary. And you'll never get him off it.

'But the thing that's really eating your dad is that he took a chance on the Lady Luck. Broke a rule he'd made when he was a young feller and had always followed. Broods about that more'n he does about the money. He'll tell you some-time—when he's ready. If he shouldn't—well—ain't much use in talking about something that's over and done with anyway.'

'I'm so glad you told me, Alec! I should have known it from his letters long ago.'

She wondered how she could have been so blind as not to realize it was more than Aunt Nina's letter that had made him so determined to give her a wonderful summer. He'd been so fearful lest the one gamble he had ever taken might affect her. If it hadn't been for that smaller cheque, she would never have guessed he was in trouble, but this she must not let him know when they talked about the reason for her coming. And they'd have to talk about it soon, she knew.

Alec lashed the tarpaulin firmly and said, 'She's stowed, and we're coming to Stephen's Passage.'

They went forward as the first of the fleet of icebergs sailed around the point. Tall and crystal-white and glistening in the sunshine, they had the airy look of creatures flying.

Judy caught her breath. 'They're lovely! I thought ice-bergs were flat and low and evil-looking.'

'That's floe ice,' Alec said. 'These are evil enough if you run into 'em. You see only a little part. They break off in big slabs and chunks from the glacier. Sounds like cannon fire when they come away. But by the time they get this far, they've lost their colour and turned over so often they're every shape you can think of.'

'Every one is different!' July watched the procession following the leader into the channel on the outgoing tide. 'Some are so beautiful! Like sculptures! I'm so glad I saw them, Alec.'

He grinned. 'I figured they'd be coming out about half tide,' he said. 'Now I'll make a pot of coffee so we'll have something hot to go with sandwiches. Then I can give the Boss a hand at the wheel.'

They ate sandwiches in the wheelhouse. It was a merry meal, and Judy thought her father made a special effort to show her he was reserving judgement until he heard her story. Afterwards they sat on the afterdeck.

'Of course, Judy, you know you can't stay here for the summer,' he said.

'But it is so silly for me to be visiting in Bar Harbour and you up here in Alaska. We haven't seen each other since last summer!'

'It was time we had a visit, although I wouldn't have suggested such a long trip for you.'

'Only a little over a week,' she said. 'In Seattle, I went right aboard the steamship from the train, and I didn't spend anywhere near all you'd sent me.' She hated to mention money, but she wanted him to know she had not been completely reckless. 'If you're worrying about Aunt Nina, I wrote her a letter on the train and sent a wire from Seattle.'

'And told her you were making only a short visit?' he asked. 'As you know, Judy, I haven't always agreed with her, but she's right about a mining camp not being the place for you.'

'I've spent vacations with you in other mining camps.'

'They were different. Mining towns in the Mother Lode in California. The Rockies in Colorado. And near cities in Nevada and Arizona. Settled country compared to a few rough shacks on a remote island in Alaska, miles from any town. Besides, you were younger—just a schoolgirl who—'

'Must have been an awful nuisance,' she broke in.

'Not at all. We've had a lot of grand times together, Judy.'

'What makes you think we wouldn't have grand times now?'

'I didn't say that,' and his tone sharpened. 'This year you should be with young people your age, friends who are facing the same problems you are. Finishing school—I'm very pleased about your grades, Judy—is a sort of—well, you've ended one phase and are entering another. You need contemporaries about you. Up here—you'd see no one except the crew and me. It's not the kind of life you need, Judy.'

'Isn't that something Aunt Nina wrote you? A sort of launching—as though I were a ship coming off the ways!'

'Let's say going into deeper waters. I like that better. I was as delighted as she over your spending the summer with the Fellows in Bar Harbour.'

'I suppose she wrote she wants to give me a coming-out party next fall.'

He nodded. 'Would you like that?'

'Perhaps.' Her tone was non-committal. 'Or I might go to college. Several of the girls are, and I thought you might like to have me go.'

'Not unless you want to, Judy.'

'I don't know what I want, except—' she hesitated—'I don't want to do anything just because everyone else is doing it. Does that make sense to you?'

He smiled. 'Not doing something for the same reason doesn't seem much more original, does it? If that was your reason for not going to Bar Harbour as we'd—'

'It wasn't!' she insisted. 'I came up here because I wanted to be with you. It's the only reason,' she went on with sudden vehemence.

'But Judy! It isn't fair to you to let you stay here. You'll understand that when you see the camp.'

'Before I've even seen the place or had more than a

glimpse of Alaska, you're already asking when I'm going to leave. What's happened to your manners? You used to have such beautiful ones.'

'Perhaps I did rush things a bit,' he admitted. 'You had me worried. It isn't like you to dash off on a four-thousand-mile journey on a sudden impulse. But now you're here—and I shouldn't have to tell you how glad I am to see you—we'll enjoy our visit and not talk about your departure until later. I only spoke of it today because I didn't want you to plan on something that I know would never do.'

'How can you know before we've even tried—' she began.

He smiled as he arose and held out a hand. 'We're coming to a fine bit of country. It's well worth seeing from the foredeck.'

They were rounding a point, and as they settled in front of the wheelhouse, the boat entered a narrow channel in the midst of mountains. Judy gasped as she looked ahead. On either side mountains rose from the sea, their glittering snow peaks reaching for the sky. Behind these peaks were others, a great welter of them, extending back and back as far as her eyes could see.

She had thought she knew mountains in the West. And the year she'd attended a school in Paris, while her father was in the African gold fields, she'd spent her Christmas holidays in Switzerland.

But these Alaskan coastal mountains were different from any she could have imagined. She was afloat on the North Pacific with peaks towering above her, and there was something incredible about a small boat winding through a flooded mountain valley. It was breath-taking in its beauty; it was awesome and, in an odd way, somehow challenging.

Her face glowing, she turned to her father. 'This is wonderful!' she cried. 'And I'm so glad my first sight of them was from a little boat below, and not far off from a big ship. Why, we're practically at their feet!'

'Not quite,' he said. 'It's a long way down to the ocean floor where they're standing.'

Judy sat entranced for hours. It was as though the country had thrown off its grey fog shroud to reveal itself in full splendour. Each short passage seemed lovelier than the one preceding. Bays and points, a sunlit sea and high sheer walls of granite. Long before the afternoon was past, she was almost drained of emotion from looking at the solid green of forests, the cloud shadows on glistening snow peaks, and the ever changing tones of bold granite shoulders embossed with lichens in subtle shadings of grey and bronze, rose and purple.

It was evening when they turned into Shaman Cove. The June sun was setting, and water, sky, forest, and the great mountain at the head of the bay were drenched in golden light.

'You never told me we had our special mountain!' she cried.

'It's more special than you know,' he said. 'If the gold we're hoping for is in that mountain, we'll have a downhill chute like the big mine in Juneau.'

The camp stood on a bench above the bay. The bunkhouse, cookhouse, power plant, and her father's small cabin, built of raw lumber, were more desolate than Judy had expected. This was nothing like the old mining camps she'd known in the West.

Sang, the Chinese cook, came to the float to carry the grocery order they had brought from Juneau. He smiled shyly when Alec introduced her, and then his face broke into a grin as Alec told him he had bought fresh meat and vegetables. The crew had eaten some time ago, but he'd kept a supper warm.

Alec carried Judy's luggage to the bedroom of the small cabin.

'It's a bit rough, Judy,' he explained. 'The Boss didn't give me much time to get things going.'

She looked at the camp bed and clothing hanging on the walls. The place was Spartan. 'But I'm taking Dad's room, Alec!' she protested.

'Sure. He can sleep in the bunkhouse until we get a place fixed for you.'

'Fixed?'

'We could run up another cabin in a hurry.'

'Did Dad plan to do that?' she asked quickly.

'There ain't been time for planning since we had your wire. I brought it in at midnight, and next day we started back to Juneau to meet the *Queen*. But don't you worry, Judy. We'll have a place for you in no time. Tell me what you want and we'll fly at it.'

'That would be wonderful!' She smiled. Apparently Alec expected her to spend the summer, or at least he hoped she would. And if Alec thought she should and there was any way of managing it, she intended to remain.

2

NEXT MORNING Judy was up early, met the crew at breakfast, and then climbed the slope to watch the drills boring into the mountain. Moving the long lines that carried air pressure was slow work, and heavy, but she sensed an excitement in the crew and even in her father, although he insisted this was only an exploration. The old need of certainties was still in complete command.

'It'll be six months at least before we'll have any idea,' he warned her.

'But you think there is a chance?'

He nodded. 'I wouldn't be here if I didn't. It's worth prospecting. Even if we feel justified in going on, it will at least be another year before we have a mine.'

'And you'll stay through the winter?' she asked.

'The company expects me to. Of course, I'll have to make a business trip to California. If I went in December, I could come east and spend Christmas with you. Missed you last year, Judy, but with things as they were at the Lady Luck, I couldn't get away. So you see my being in Alaska isn't going to mean we won't see each other.'

'It hasn't so far,' Judy said, and he laughed. Then he wasn't really upset about her change in summer plans. Yesterday she had thought he might be.

That afternoon she discarded Alec's idea of a separate cabin and began to work on a plan of adding to the present one. They could have two bedrooms with a living room between. She didn't show her sketch to her father, and when Alec asked her about it, she told him there was no hurry.

'Dad says he doesn't mind sleeping in the bunkhouse,' she said.

'It was you I was thinking of,' Alec said. 'You'd feel more settled if you had a place of your own.'

In the next few days David Randolph didn't speak of her departure or refer again to the Lady Luck. At times she thought he was making a special effort to avoid this subject. But they talked of many other things, talked through the long evenings with a late sunset drenching their little cove in flaming colour. Spoke of things they'd never talked about before because they'd really had no opportunity to discover one another. And perhaps because of what Alec had told her of her father's self-reproach about the Lady Luck, she had the feeling they were closer than they'd ever been.

She had never known much about her father's youth, except from Aunt Nina who regarded her brother as a sweet and delightful person with a strange passion for the history of the earth's beginnings. And now she found her father's stories of his college years absorbing. The evening he told her how he happened to become a geologist through a chance course he had taken, she was fascinated.

'It's a strange thing how the genius of one man can suddenly fire you,' he finished. 'There I was, a feckless sort of student, with no special interests, only going to college because it was the thing to do. And after the first lecture I never wanted to be anything but a geologist and mining engineer. It was decided in that one hour.' He looked at the clock on his desk. 'Good heavens!' he exclaimed. 'It's nearly midnight, and I've been running on since supper. Must have had a lot of words bottled up in me. You'll be worn out before your visit's over, but when you go back, don't tell Nina that I've kept you up half the night reminiscing.'

Next morning Judy finished her plan of the larger cabin and showed it to Alec.

He studied it, then smiled broadly. 'Just the ticket!' he exclaimed. 'Something big enough for the two of you.'

'Would it be much to build?' she asked with some trepidation.

'What if it is? The Boss ain't had any comfort in this place! And he's got it coming to him. I'll take a couple of lads off the job and set 'em at it. Have it done in no time.'

'We'll put in some bookshelves. He likes books around

him.' She considered a fireplace, then decided not to mention it. That could come later.

'And some easy chairs,' Alec added. 'Neal Davis, that young fellow in the power plant crew, is handy with tools. Could build anything you need. How about some little tables?'

'They'd be wonderful for lamps,' she said. 'And could we add a wardrobe with a chest of drawers to Dad's bedroom? Give him a place to keep his clothes.'

'Easy!' Alec folded the plan and put it in his pocket. 'I'll get right at it. Bet the Boss liked this idea.'

'I haven't told him yet. I will tonight.'

She spoke with far more confidence than she felt, but they couldn't go on forever with nothing decided about her staying. At least planning and furnishing a cabin would be one answer to his objection that there was nothing for her to do in Shaman Cove. She'd be busy, and suddenly it occurred to her that never before had she had a part in the making of a home. She felt a little thrill of anticipation, was still glowing with it when her father entered the office.

'How about it, Alec?' he asked. 'Trust me with the *Working Stiff* to run to Rampart Bay? I want to see that young fellow who has a freight line.'

'Guess you could make it. Not much breeze and I can show you how to start and stop the engine.'

'Want to come with me, Judy?' her father asked.

'I'd love to—that is, if Alec thinks it's safe.'

David Randolph grinned. 'It's only twelve miles up the shore. Chart shows it just inside Falcon Inlet. I met the manager of the cannery when we were in Juneau, and he told me Rampart Bay was a steamship stop and there's a young chap who delivers mail and freight around here.'

'Baird's his name,' Alec said. 'He could save us that long slog to Juneau. But how about our cables?'

'Mr. Daniels said to have them forwarded to the cannery with theirs. He's a pleasant chap. You'll like him, Judy. I promised to drop in the first time I went to Rampart Bay.'

The day promised a real adventure, and she started for the bedroom. 'I'll be dressed and ready in a minute.'

'No need to change for—' her father began.

'It won't take her half as long as it will Sang to tell me what the cook camp needs in case there's a store around there. Must be one at the cannery. Sang's been brooding about our running low on canned meat, which he doesn't think much of anyway. It's my guess he's looking for an excuse to go hunting.'

Alec saw them off. They went out in the Strait and turned North. The day was lovely, with just enough breeze to make the small waves dance and sparkle in the sunlight. Far ahead a line of snow peaks hung in the sky like great white clouds. Judy stood in the door of the wheelhouse revelling in their beauty and thinking too how nearly she had missed this new and exciting country. But for that sudden impulse she might now have been with Marcia Fellows in Bar Harbour, doing the same things she'd done so many summers. Then gradually she became aware of her father staring at her. She had the feeling he'd been watching her a long time.

She turned and smiled at him. 'Every minute I'm more glad than ever I came up here,' she said, and there was a challenge in her voice.

For a moment she thought he wasn't going to answer as he glanced at the compass and lined up a point ahead. Then he looked at her sharply.

'What decided you to come, Judy? The cheque I sent you —only half of what I'd promised—and my having to tell you I couldn't send the rest until later?'

'It was far more than I needed—more than I'd ever—' She stopped. She should have known he would have guessed the reason for her sudden decision. 'Look, Dad,' she said earnestly. 'It was enough to get me to Alaska—where— where I really wanted to be.'

'Because you thought I was in trouble—that I couldn't afford your Bar Harbour summer. I knew that was what brought you dashing up here. Knew it all along.'

'It wasn't—' she began, then saw his disbelieving smile. 'At least, it wasn't the only reason.'

'I imagine Alec has already told you, but I'd intended to tell you anyway. It's time we had this straight between us.

I took a beating on the Lady Luck. It was my own fault. I asked for that jolt. But things aren't desperate enough to spoil your summer. And I'd like to pay for my own folly, without feeling it had touched you.'

'Why shouldn't it touch me, Dad?' she asked. 'After all —you and I—why, we're all the family each other has.'

Suddenly his eyes were very tender. 'That was a wonderful thing to say, Judy. Something I will remember, always.' He steered for a moment in silence. 'The reason I asked you to come with me today was that I wanted to tell you I can well afford your Bar Harbour summer. Swing it easily. When we've had our visit, why not go back there? You can write Marcia Fellows this afternoon while we're in Rampart Bay. Or better yet, send a cable.'

'So that's what you've been planning the last few days!' She laughed. 'You're out of luck, Dad. With half the school just waiting for an invitation, her guest list will be filled by now. I knew that when I told her I was going to Alaska. And I'm not the least bit sorry.'

'Burned your bridges, did you? Out of desperation?'

'Not at all! I wanted to be with you.' Now that the matter of the Lady Luck was behind them, she had the feeling he might believe her. 'Besides,' she added, 'a summer in Alaska would be different—and rather wonderful.'

'Alaska, yes, if you were going to see the country! But not a mining camp on a lonely coast. Your Aunt Nina's right! It's no place for you, Judy. Not this summer. Weeks, months, shut off from everything, and no touch with the outside world. Nothing to fill your days. I can't let you—'

'There's plenty for me to do,' she broke in vehemently. His smile was sceptical. 'Of course there is! Alec and I have already planned something that will keep me busy for weeks and weeks. We're going to build a decent place for you to live.'

'You mean a house?' he demanded, and she nodded. 'Oh, no, Judy,' he said quickly. 'I'm sorry, but we're not ready for houses yet. I can't let the company spend money it doesn't have to, until we're sure of what we have here.'

'But this would cost them hardly anything! Just two

rooms added to your cabin. Alec said he could run it up in no time. Neal Davis can build all the furniture we need, and I can do the painting and add little extras to make it liveable. It's a crime the way you've had to spend evening after evening in that tiny office without a decent chair. Why, even the crew has a place in the bunkhouse where they can play cards and talk in comfort.'

'Ever paint before?'

'No, but I've wanted to. Lots of women do. You told me yourself how Mother always fixed up the places where you lived in the old mining camps.'

He smiled. 'She could take a pot of paint, a couple of orange crates, and a few yards of calico and transform an old shack into a real home, Judy. It was amazing.'

'How she must have loved doing it,' Judy said. 'I know because right now I'm bursting with ideas about that cabin. And you need it, Dad, staying up here through the winter. Is it all right to go ahead?'

'If you mean only an addition to the present cabin, that sounds great, Judy! Are you going to add a second bed-room?'

'Yes, and a living-room so that you can be comfortable in the evenings.'

'How long does Alec think the job will take?'

'He said two men could build it in no time. Of course—my part—dressing it up afterwards will take much longer. But,' and she looked at him tentatively, 'there's no need for me to hurry since I'm not going to Bar Harbour, and it doesn't make any difference to Aunt Nina when I get to Martha's Vineyard. I'll write her I'm staying on a bit.'

'But you will assure her that when we've had our visit and this building spree is over, you are returning to the East, won't you?'

She laughed. 'Are you that scared of Aunt Nina?'

'Always have been,' he confessed. 'Why not? A mining engineer, always on the move, no settled home and a girl child to raise. Bound to make a lot of boners.'

'Not that I've noticed. I've rather admired you as a parent.'

Her father was startled for a moment, then his face broke into smiles. 'Why, Judy!' he exclaimed. 'Have you really? I doubt if Nina will be of the same opinion when she hears you're staying on awhile.'

'Aunt Nina!' and Judy laughed. 'Why she'd be shocked, Dad, if I didn't stay for a real visit after coming all this way. It wouldn't make sense. When I write to her about the cabin and that you're to have a decent home this winter, she'll be delighted.'

He swung closer to the western shore. A mountain ridge rose beside them. Half-way up, the forest gave way to steep bare cliffs, where long tongues of delicate green shrubs and moss climbed in the crevices. Judy was thinking what a lovely pattern they made when her father spoke.

'If that point ahead is the entrance to Falcon Inlet, we're nearing Rampart Bay.'

Judy looked at the chart. 'Baird Light!' she said. 'Didn't Alec say Baird was the name of the man you want to see?'

'Yes. Spencer Baird. It seems he's something of a local hero. He discovered the reef, forced the govenment to put in a light, and saved the town as a steamship stop. Daniels said it was a tricky passage even for small boats.'

They turned into Falcon Inlet. Before them, between two great cliffs standing in the sea like an open gate, lay the entrance to Rampart Bay. As they passed through the narrow channel, the exhaust of the *Working Stiff* echoed 'and re-echoed off the walls like a bombardment. When the clamour had died down, Judy stared at the half circle of the bay. A few buildings straggled along the west shore to a sawmill at the head. Across the bay was the cannery. Everywhere, timbered mountains rose sheerly from the beach.

'Are we going to call on Mr Daniels?' Judy asked.

'Later. First I want to find this young Baird who owns the freight boat. I imagine that's his float in front of the store.'

As they approached, Judy saw a young man carrying boxes into the freight shed of the float and wondered if he were the local hero. David Randolph closed the throttle to come alongside, but when he pulled the lever to release the clutch, he could not budge it.

'Look out, Judy!' he yelled. 'We're going to crash!'

He turned the wheel frantically, and the bow just missed the float, but the starboard side struck and scraped along it. The young man dashed out of the freight shed and leaped aboard just as the stern passed. He ran forward to the wheelhouse.

'I can't budge this lever!' Randolph shouted.

'Your clutch is frozen,' the stranger said.

He took the wheel, brought the *Working Stiff* around in a big circle. Then for the first time he seemed to be aware of Judy standing in the wheelhouse door. His eyes widened. Then he smiled.

'Hello,' she said. 'And thank you.'

She was still shaken at the thought of what might have happened if this competent young man hadn't taken charge of them, but not so shaken as not to notice his unusually attractive smile. There was a glint in his keen grey eyes, and she'd always liked dark men. Altogether, there was quite an air about him, and she didn't wonder that he was a local hero.

'That was quick thinking,' her father said. 'Another second and you couldn't have boarded us. I'm David Randolph.' He thrust out a hand. 'And this is my daughter, Judy.'

'I've heard you'd opened up at Shaman Cove,' the other said as they shook hands. 'I'm Rod Baird.'

'Not Spencer?' David Randolph asked.

'Spence is my brother. He's out in the *Taku* on his freight run.'

The *Working Stiff* was again nearing the float. Rod turned off the ignition. 'The headway will take us in,' he said, and as the boat drifted gently against the float, Rod jumped ashore and made the lines fast.

'Were you frightened?' he asked as he helped Judy off.

'Not after you leaped aboard. Before that I didn't have time to be much of anything—not even useful.' She laughed. 'I wonder if Dad or I would ever have thought to shut off the ignition.'

'Sure you would,' Rod said and turned to her father. 'I

expected you'd be along soon. There's mail here for you.'

'Already? I left the forwarding order in Juneau only a few days ago.'

'Must have been in time to catch this week's boat. There's quite a bundle for you at the store.'

He led the way up the ramp and across the beach. The store stood on a slight rise and was evidently an old dwelling. As they entered, Judy stared with astonishment at the large, bright shop with well-filled shelves.

'I say!' her father exclaimed. 'You boys have a real store here!'

Rod smiled with pleasure. 'Thank you, sir,' he said. 'I'll get your mail.'

Judy watched him cross to the cubbyholes in the corner. Somehow she hadn't expected a young Alaskan to use the deferential 'sir' to an older man. Rod handed the packet of letters to her father, who shuffled through them quickly.

'There are several I should answer. When is your next outgoing mail?' he asked.

'Day after tomorrow. The *Resolute* calls in once a week. You can write your letters in my office.' He led the way to the small office in the rear, cleared the desk, and laid out paper and envelopes.

David Randolph read the printed letterhead. 'Rampart Bay Store, Chichagoff Island. Roderick Baird, Proprietor.' 'I see,' he said. 'Your brother owns the freight boat and you have the store.'

'Yes. I took it over two years ago when the fellow who ran it wanted to get out.'

David Randolph glanced at him. 'A bit young for a store-keeper, weren't you?'

'I was sixteen. And the salmon trollers had to have another store beside the cannery's.'

'Is there anyone around here who can fix that clutch?'

'Tom Walsh is a good mechanic,' Rod said. 'His boat works are just up the shore. I can tow you. Or'—and he glanced at Judy—'we can walk across the point and tell him to get the boat.'

'Let's walk,' she said. 'Wouldn't that be simpler?'

They were at the door when her father called, 'Hey, Rod, wait a minute! What if you have a customer?'

'I won't,' Rod said. 'The trollers don't get in till evening.'

As they started across the trail, Judy asked where the trollers lived. She'd been wondering about a store in an almost empty bay. 'I mean,' she said, 'I don't see many houses.'

'They live on their boats and tie up overnight. A few are in here every evening, but when king salmon are really running, the float is jammed. Moored so close they can step from one boat to another. It's quite a sight. A regular troller town.' There was a note of pride in his voice. 'You see,' he went on, 'trolling is a lonely business, and they like to get together in the evening.' He glanced at her curiously. 'Know anything about commercial fishing?'

'A little. I spent a summer at Cape Cod. But those fishermen live ashore with their families.'

'A troller has to go where king salmon are running, and they stay out as long as they can take the weather.'

'Mr Daniels told Dad that the canneries were open only a few months in summer.'

'Sure. Alaskan canneries don't pack king salmon. Trollers sell the kings to salteries. Daniels hasn't opened yet.'

She looked across at the cannery buildings strung along the shore. At the end of the point was a huddle of small cabins.

'Who lives in those?' she asked.

'Tlingit Indians. They come in every summer to work at the cannery. Now they're waiting, just like Daniels and every canner in south-eastern Alaska, for the run of pinks.'

'The run of pinks?' she repeated.

'The pink salmon. It's a different species to the king, but it's the pinks that make the salmon canning business the biggest thing in Alaska. Bigger even than our gold mines —and a lot more exciting. That is, when you know about them.'

She glanced at him, startled. His voice had taken on a vibrant timbre, and there was an earnestness about him she hadn't sensed before.

'Pinks spawn in these rivers,' he went on, 'and come back to spawn in their home stream. Millions and millions of them come back in summer. We don't know where they come from. All we know is that the young leave the rivers, go out to sea, stay two years, and then return to spawn and die in that same river. That's the pink run everybody's waiting for right now. It happens suddenly. One week there won't be a pink in the country. And then the next they're here! Hundreds and hundreds of thousands of them coming back from somewhere at sea. For weeks and months they keep on coming! Filling the rivers! Sometimes it seems there's more fish than water. You can't believe it. You'd swear there wasn't another two-year-old pink in the world. And still they come! Crowding against the current, fighting rapids, even jumping up steep falls to get upstream to spawning grounds. Millions and millions of them!'

She drew in her breath. 'I'd love to see a run,' she said.

'Would you?' His tone quickened. 'How long will you be up here?'

'All summer,' and then she added quickly, 'at least I hope so.'

'Fine! Next month when they're running right I'll show you a river. It's something—well—until you've seen it, you can't believe it.'

'It must be sort of—of overwhelming—like your mountains.' She studied him a moment. 'You know I never would have guessed you were a fisherman.'

'I'm not.' He looked at her in amazement. 'I never even wanted to be. Oh, when I was a kid, I worked on a purse seiner for part of a season. Hated it every minute.'

'Then why—' she began.

'You mean the way I sounded off about the pink run?' He laughed. 'That was only an Alaskan boasting about his country. I don't do it often. Honest!'

'But I liked it!'

'Did you? Really?' His eyes lighted. 'Maybe it wasn't all boasting. You don't have to boast about a country that's got what this has.'

'Were you born here?'

27

'Might as well have been. Came up with my family when I was six and lived at the head of Falcon Inlet until I took over the store.' They had come out on a little cove. Rod pointed to a shed. 'There's the boat works. Doesn't look like much, but Tom Walsh has built some fine boats there.'

Tom came out to meet them. Rod introduced Judy and explained their errand.

'Sounds like a frozen cone clutch,' Tom said.

'Will it take long to fix?' Judy asked.

'Depends on what I find. Maybe two hours. Maybe half a day.' He started for his tug. 'You folks want to ride back with me?'

'We'll walk, and beat you there,' Rod said, and as they started down the trail, he laughed. 'I wasn't taking any chances on being held up an hour talking to his wife. Mary Walsh was at the floathouse door, just waiting to meet the girl from outside.'

'How would she know I was from the outside?'

Rod grinned. 'Same way we know the difference between a yacht and a work boat two miles off.' He looked at her with frank admiration.

Judy blushed, and then she laughed. She'd never been likened to a yacht before, but she found it a refreshing way of showing male approval, and Rod was a comfortable person to be with. She was surprised at how much she told him about herself on the walk back—things she didn't ordinarily tell people she didn't know well. Strangers, she'd discovered, were apt to consider her lack of a fixed home either delightfully eccentric or somewhat pitiful. But Rod didn't appear to think it was at all astonishing that she had spent a Christmas holiday in the mountains of Switzerland, knew the Atlantic coastline well, and had visited mining camps in Colorado and California. He was only amazed that so seasoned a traveller had never before come to Alaska.

They were waiting on the float when Tom Walsh arrived in his tug. After the first glance Tom said the trouble was a frozen clutch, and if it were sprung, the job would take half a day at least. The best they could hope for would be the middle of the afternoon. 'If I run into real grief, it will be later,' he warned Judy as he departed.

She watched the crippled *Working Stiff* being towed away and hoped the trouble wouldn't be serious. Back at the store she reported all this to her father, who accepted the news calmly. Judy suspected he would never be a really earnest motor boat skipper and decided to ask Alec to show her how to run the *Working Stiff*. Then she could do the mine's errands.

David Randolph was still writing letters. He handed Sang's list to Judy. 'Can you and Rod take care of this?' he asked. 'You'd be better at it than I am, anyway. Alec's always run the cook camp.'

And this, she thought, was another job she could take off Alec's overloaded shoulders. What made Aunt Nina and her father think there was nothing for her to do at a mining camp?

Judy looked at the list. 'Sang's made a point of canned meat. Beef especially.'

'That's easy,' Rod said. 'I always have it for the trollers. They need a meal in a hurry and don't want to fuss with cooking fresh meat.'

'Do you have that too?'

'Yes. And fruit and vegetables, every week on boat day. Those things go fast, but I can save some for you when the *Resolute* gets in day after tomorrow. After that I'll order what you want.'

'Wonderful!' she said. 'Sang has been a bit morose about supplies. What can I tell him he will have this week?'

Rod brought out his order sheet. 'Head lettuce, tomatoes, asparagus, carrots, oranges, beef for steak or roasts, and maybe strawberries.'

'Fresh ones?'

'How big is the crew?'

'Fourteen,' she said, 'besides Dad and me.'

'Then don't mention strawberries. I couldn't hold out enough from the sawmill order. All old-timers in that crew, and you know how they feel about nothing being too good for an Alaskan.'

'I never heard that!'

'You will, though. It's the motto all Alaskans are brought up on.'

She knew he was joking but half-serious too and wondered if perhaps that didn't explain a certain manner she'd noticed in Alaskans. She'd been aware of it on shipboard even before she had reached Juneau. It wasn't arrogance, but their bearing carried a buoyant sense of pride and confidence. She'd rather admired it and envied it a bit too.

They finished Sang's order and added a few items he hadn't thought of. The counter was piled high.

'And now for my list,' she said. 'We're going to enlarge Dad's cabin, and I'll need paint and material for curtains and pillows and chair covers. Something to liven up the room for winter.'

'All I carry is stuff for Indian women's dresses. It's pretty dreary. Nothing you'd want to look at day after day.'

'I thought all Indians liked red.'

'That's what lots of people think, and maybe some tribes do, but Tlingit women want dark colours. I can order material from Juneau. Or better yet—here's a catalogue. It's mail order, but I can get it for you if you tell me how many yards you need.'

'I don't know,' she said. 'I'll have to find out from Alec what furniture we'll have. He's the man who—' She hesitated. She'd never been quite sure how to describe his status.

'You mean the straw boss who came up to get the camp started,' Rod said, and when she looked surprised, he added, 'I've heard a lot about him. And about your father. But nobody mentioned you.'

'How could they? Even Dad didn't know I was coming until just in time to meet the ship at Juneau. I was lucky he ever got my cable.'

'Made up your mind to come and started, did you?' He laughed. 'But you wouldn't have had any trouble even if they hadn't met you. You'd have come to Rampart on the *Resolute*, and we'd have seen you got to Shaman Cove.'

She smiled. The 'we' was obviously Rod and his motor boat. 'And wouldn't Dad and Alec have been surprised if I'd suddenly dropped in,' she said, almost wishing it had happened that way. 'Can I take this catalogue with me and let you know what I need later? And of course you have paint?'

'For boats. White, grey, green, and mast colour—that's a sort of yellow tan. Better take this colour card along with the catalogue. Allow two weeks to fill the order, but you won't need any of this before then.'

'You don't know Alec! He'll have the cabin finished long before then, but I'll do the painting later.' She found this idea enormously intriguing. As her glance travelled down the rows of colour patches, she toyed with all sorts of exciting possibilities. 'With these mountains and all this colour, an Alaskan cabin could be so lovely,' she said.

Rod was packing the groceries when David Randolph came out of the office with his letters.

'Finished?' And he nodded with approval. 'I was sure, Judy, your Aunt Nina must have taught you how to run a household.'

'But she never dreamed it would be a mining camp with a Chinese cook who doesn't speak English. At least not to me. I'll have to ask Alec how he manages.'

'I can teach you a fine sign language,' Rod said. 'It works with my Tlinget customers.'

'And now about our credit—' David Randolph began.

'The Northwest Mining Corporation, isn't it?' Rod asked. 'Shall I send the bill to you at Shaman Cove?' He waited for the other's nod, then went on, 'And now if everybody is as hungry as I am, I'll cook a lunch. Bacon and eggs are one of my stand-bys. I hope you people like them.'

ℬ

ROD'S LIVING QUARTERS, a kitchen and small bedroom, were behind the store. Judy noticed the kitchen was clean, but not fussy clean, only the way a man might keep it. Rod built the fire, set the table, and started to fry the bacon.

'Shall I make eggs *brouillés*?' she asked. 'It's one of the few things I do well, and Dad likes them. All I need is a bowl, a double boiler, and a wooden spoon, if you happen to have one.'

He produced all three, then watched as she stirred the creamy mass. 'That's how Vicky always did it,' he said. 'Only she called them scrambled eggs.'

'Exactly what they are, but at Aunt Nina's they were known as eggs *brouillés*. Who is Vicky?'

'My sister. She's living in New York. At least, I call it New York. She says it's The Village.'

'Greenwich Village?' Judy asked.

'Yes. She's married to an artist.'

For a moment Judy thought he'd intended to be dramatic, then realized that to him this amazing statement was only something that might be expected of any Alaskan. A score of questions flitted through her mind, but she fell back on an indirect one.

'Oh,' she said, 'Then she didn't live in Falcon Inlet?'

'She did until she married, two years ago. Phil Trent—he's her husband and a grand fellow—came up here on that expedition in the Craig yacht, the *Cytherea*.'

David Randolph looked up. 'You mean the group of scientists Amos Craig brought to Alaska? I saw one of their reports.'

'The one on fish,' Rod said. 'The fellow who wrote it sent it to me. It was good.'

'I understand there will be others.'

Rod nodded. 'On the glaciers and the Tlingit Indians.'

'And that's how Vicky met her husband!' Judy exclaimed, beginning to feel solid ground beneath her.

'Oh, she and Phil had known each other ever since the summer Phil chartered Spence's boat for a trip and Vicky went along as mate. She was sixteen then. So when Phil came up again on Craig's yacht, he brought the gang in to ask her to go to Muir Glacier with them.' He laughed. 'They came back from Muir all set to go to New York together, and they couldn't believe that I wasn't surprised when they told me.'

David Randolph filled in the silence. 'There was a photograph of the *Cytherea* in the report. She must be a beautiful yacht.'

'She is,' Rod said fervently. 'A hundred and fifty footer, and the finest that ever came to Alaska. Carries a crew of twenty-two.'

'Was it a large party?' Judy asked.

'Only seven. Mr Craig and his daughter, four scientists, and Phil, the photographer. Vicky took pictures too, and Mr Craig is using some of them in the booklet he's going to print about the cruise. Tickled her a lot. She's studying photography. Under a fellow by the name of Streeter.'

'Not Ernest Streeter!' Judy exclaimed. 'Why, he's an artist too! He gave a talk to the art class at school, and everyone thought he was wonderful!'

'So does Vicky. Funny you should happen to know someone Vicky knows.'

It did seem to have brought their worlds much closer. Rod must have felt this too because he went on to talk more freely of Vicky and of his family. Vicky was twenty and in between Spence and himself. When they were younger, Spence and Vicky had teamed up, and it was only in her last year at home, when she helped in the store occasionally, that he'd really got to know her.

'You'd like her,' and he looked at Judy. 'She and Phil expected to be here this summer, but now they're waiting for a young man who's coming. Have him named already. Jefferson Baird Trent, after my father. And is Jeff set up about it! He's already planning on the things they'll do together next year. It wouldn't surprise me if he'd want to take the youngster out to kill a big brownie.'

'Did your father like Vicky marrying a stranger and going so far away—to New York?' Judy asked. She'd been curious about this, and Rod's casual references to the marriage hadn't filled in many basic facts.

'Not right at first,' Rod said, and he was suddenly rather sober. 'You see—Jeff has his own ideas about some things. Well'—he paused, evidently searching for the right words—'you'll understand it better when you know him. But afterwards he was all for it, and for Phil too.' He broke off a piece of toast, buttered it slowly, then looked up. 'In some ways Vicky's going off to New York was the best thing that ever happened to Jeff. I can remember when Jeff never thought of mail day, but now he's down to meet the boat every week. Vicky's being in New York shook him loose from a few notions.'

Judy was hoping he'd go on. She had found this marriage of Vicky's to a New York artist fascinating, but almost as though he regretted having revealed so much, Rod had turned to her father.

'Judy said you wanted to call on Daniels. I can take you over while your clutch is being fixed.'

'But first we're going to wash these dishes,' Judy announced firmly. He started to protest. 'There's plenty of time. Bring out your dishpan.'

They found Mr Daniels in his office, where Rod left them, after arranging to pick them up when the repairs on the *Working Stiff* were finished.

Judy liked the canner, although her father's phrase, 'a pleasant chap', was not the one she would have chosen. He was very friendly, but she sensed a driving force underneath his affability. Perhaps it hadn't been so evident in Juneau, but here with the whole crew working at top speed to put the cannery in running condition, his intensity was unmistakable. He was interrupted a dozen times by workmen asking for his orders.

'Sorry,' he said, 'but we have to get this place going before the pink run,' Judy nodded, glad she now knew that 'pink run' meant salmon. 'And we can't tell when it will happen,' the canner went on. 'First we'll know is when they show in the traps.'

'Traps! Is that how you catch them?' her father asked.

'Yes. And without traps, salmon packing would never have become Alaska's biggest industry.'

'More than gold?' David Randolph questioned.

'I'd say so. Last year, Alaska's salmon pack brought over thirty million dollars on the market. The industry has grown tremendously. In 1900 there were only sixteen canneries in south-eastern Alaska. Now, only fourteen years later, there are forty-five. And it's the floating traps that, in the main, supply the fish to keep all these canneries operating.'

'Who sets them?' David Randolph asked. 'The canner?'

Mr Daniels chuckled. 'I wish it were as easy as you make it sound. A trap is a real property. First a canner must prospect for a site, where it is reasonably certain the fish will run. And good sites are becoming rare now. Then he must obtain a licence for the site from the government, at a fee, of course. All this before he can start to build the trap, which will cost him anything up to ten thousand dollars.'

'But what do these traps look like?' Judy asked. 'Have we seen any?'

'You may have and not recognized them. All that shows above the surface is a framework of heavy timbers with a little shack built on it. The trap itself hangs from those timbers. It's—well—let's say it's a big oblong bag of steel webbing. Of course there's a lot more to it, but this will give you the general idea. And running from this bag to shore is a hanging wall of wire webbing, which leads the fish into the trap where we can brail them and take—'

'Brail?' David Randolph asked quickly, then smiled as he added, 'Remember Judy and I are still tenderfeet.'

'It's a heavy net stretched between two poles or brails,' the canner explained. 'We slip that under the fish in the trap, and lift them into the tender to take them to the cannery.'

'I should have figured that out from the word.' David

Randolph laughed. 'Now I hesitate to ask you what the little shack on top is for.'

'The trap watchman. He lives in it. He has to see that the trap is working, keep the webbing clean, and make sure no one steals our fish. No other canner would, of course, but some purse seiners make a business of fish-pirating. They like nothing better than to raid a trap, then sell the fish back to their rightful owner. And once they're in the purse seiner, there's no proof of where they caught the salmon.' He forestalled the question on Judy's lips. 'A purse seiner is exactly what the word says. When the fishermen find a good school of salmon, they run a long, deep net around it, then pull a rope that draws the bottom together just like a purse.'

'Oh,' she said. 'I wondered. Rod told me he had worked on a purse seiner but didn't like it.'

'He didn't?' Mr Daniels' tone sharpened. 'Did he happen to tell you what boat? Was is it by any chance the *Sea Lion*?'

'He didn't tell me the name, but—'

'It's not important,' the canner assured her quickly. 'Just curiosity on my part. I'd heard he'd got a job at Wrangell that summer he quit the *Taku*.'

Judy flushed. Mr Daniels had said it wasn't important, and yet she had the feeling that perhaps she shouldn't have spoken of it.

Mr Daniels turned to her father. 'Were you able to get Spence to handle your mail and freight?'

'Rod said he was sure Spence would do it. I'm grateful to you for telling me about him. It's quite an unusual family, but I suppose there are a lot of them, tucked off in odd corners on this coast.'

'Not families. A few old Klondikers. Left-overs from the gold rush. Had one of them in Rampart Bay. Lived where the Baird store is now. Spent years poking around Chichagoff, sure there was gold on this island. I thought of him when I heard you people had opened up at Shaman Cove. It would break his heart if you ran into something big.'

'I suppose it would,' David Randolph said. 'I hadn't

understood that this Baird family were left-overs from—'

'No. Jeff Baird is different from those old fellows. He sailed his family up here years ago, when the kids were youngsters. He wasn't hunting gold or salmon, or even a fresh start in life apparently. What he was looking for was frontier country, an empty inlet with plenty of game and mountains and no neighbours nearer than fifteen miles. He's a wonderful hunter and the finest axeman I ever knew. He wasn't satisfied with an ordinary cabin but built a big log house that's quite impressive. I hired him to get spruce piling for this wharf and timbers for the traps, and he put the stuff into the water faster than a whole crew could have done it ordinarily. Kept two pile drivers busy. So you see he isn't lazy.'

'Where did the children go to school?' Judy asked.

'They didn't. Their mother taught them. She was a school teacher and is really a remarkable woman. My daughter was very much impressed by her when she visited them at Hidden Harbour. And by the way, Chris may be here this summer. One of our owners, Jim Richards, comes in his yacht several times a season, and if his wife is with him, Chris might join them. Will you be here through the summer?'

'We hadn't quite decided.' Judy glanced at her father. 'But I know I'll be here for some time.'

'I was thinking if Chris came while you were still here, you might spend a few days on the *Chasima*. They live aboard during the Rampart stay, and Mrs Richards enjoys having young people with her.'

'I'd love to,' Judy said. 'Does Chris come to Rampart Bay often?'

'Hasn't for several years. A cannery in the packing season is no place for a family. We packers go at top speed from the time the pink run starts, and there's nothing for Chris to do around here.'

'So I've been telling Judy,' David Randolph said. 'I'm afraid she'll find Shaman Cove very lonely, wonderful as it is to have a visit from her. We haven't seen each other since last August.'

37

The canner nodded. 'You mining engineers are even greater rovers than salmon packers. By the way, I hope you told the office at Juneau to give your cables to the cannery boat. Shall I send them to the store for Spence to deliver?'

'I'd be most grateful if you did,' David Randolph said. 'But we don't want to be a nuisance.'

'Glad to do it, and you can be sure Spence will see you get them promptly. He's dependable, and a real boatman. That lad is going places.'

'And so will Rod, I imagine, from what we saw of him this morning,' David Randolph said.

'Rod?' The canner smiled. 'I know him too, gave him his first job. He said he was sixteen. Of course I knew he wasn't, but he was a bright lad and I needed a timekeeper and someone to tend the company store. We don't sell much, and don't really want to, although we have to keep tobacco and clothing for the crew and supplies for seiners.' Obviously he was telling them in the nicest way possible that the cannery had no time to bother with a mining camp's orders, but Judy, remembering Rod's speech about the trollers needing some store beside the cannery's, had difficulty not to smile. 'The trouble with Rod,' the canner said, 'was that he couldn't believe I meant it or that I knew my business.'

'Have other ideas?' David Randolph laughed.

'Too many! He's clever all right. That's his trouble. Never had a boss, and doesn't want one. I had to let him go finally. In another six months he'd have been taking over my job. Of course he was just a cocky kid, and probably being Jeff's son had something to do with it. The old boy is rather arrogant in his opinions, but I understand he's mellowed somewhat since Vicky has been living in New York.'

'Is her husband nice?' Judy asked.

'I didn't meet him. Nor Amos Craig. I was busy packing fish when the *Cytherea* was in here. But all Rampart was stirred up for weeks, and Chris was quite excited to think of Vicky married to an artist and living in Greenwich Village.'

'And so was I, when Rod told us,' Judy confessed. 'It's—it's so unexpected. Did the girls know each other very well?'

'Chris liked Vicky and the whole family. She even thought their life in Hidden Harbour was wonderful. I believe the girls still keep track of each other. Chris is sure this Trent is a coming artist and says he's already selling pictures.'

'Really! I'm so glad! How exciting for a girl who'd never known anything except a little inlet in Alaska. Why—it's like a fairy tale!'

Mr Daniels chuckled. 'That's what Chris said.'

And it was, Judy thought. Only so seldom it came true. If it hadn't been for Amos Craig and his expedition and so many other things. She was still thinking how narrowly the two had come to missing one another when a workman entered the office.

'Rod's waiting at the wharf,' he said. 'And your boat is fixed.'

David Randolph stood up quickly. 'And we ought to get started. Alec will be wondering what's happened to us. He's the real boss around our camp,' he explained to the canner. 'I'm still dreading having to tell him about that clutch.'

As they crossed the bay in Rod's motor boat, Judy watched him at the wheel and tried to make all the stories of the Bairds fit together. The pictures of them were so different—the canner's reservations, Chris's more romantic impressions, and the things Rod had told them about himself and the family. Nor could she believe Rod was cocky and oversure of himself. He hadn't shown it, although there was a challenging set to his shoulders and an air of knowing what he was about. And why not? He'd proved his right to his own opinion about the need of a trollers' store, and now after she'd heard the other side of the story, she could understand the pride in Rod's voice when he talked about his troller town, and realize too that it wasn't just a store but a community centre which filled a real need on an empty coast.

Tom Walsh was waiting on the float to demonstrate how a cone clutch should be handled. Judy suspected the lesson was completely wasted, but her father was grateful, if still somewhat puzzled. Rod stowed the grocery order in the

Working Stiff's small cabin, and the Randolphs were ready to depart.

'You'll tell Spence to put us on his route,' her father said as Rod threw off their lines.

'First thing tomorrow morning,' Rod called. 'See you later.'

Rod didn't tell Spence the next morning. It wasn't until the day after when the weekly steamship was almost due that Spence rushed into the store with a big sack of mail.

'Where's Henry Dane? I've got to get these into the mail-sack for the *Resolute*,' he said.

'Cutting things pretty fine these days, aren't you?' Rod asked by way of congratulation. Spence looked tired but so cheerful that Rod knew he must have had a big trip. The harder Spence was driven, the better he liked it. 'Where have you been this time?'

'I picked up an extra job, a run to the mainland, but coming back I had to buck the flood up the Strait.'

'Bet that broke your heart. All those extra drops of gasoline!' Spence's mania for using tide instead of fuel was an old joke between them. 'Henry locked the mail sack an hour ago, but he ought to be around here somewhere.'

'He ought to be, but is he?'

'Keep your shirt on, feller. I'll get him for you.'

He opened the door and yelled, and a moment later Henry appeared to unlock the mail sack with what was for him real alacrity. Rod grinned at Spence and motioned him into the office.

'Got a new freighting job for you. The mining camp at Shaman Cove. Want weekly service. Nice people too. The girl and her father were in here the other day.'

'Girl!'

'Sure. David Randolph's daughter. I think she's going to be here all summer.'

Spence was still staring in amazement. 'But Randolph's a big name in—'

'Sure. And she's a peach. Reminds you of Vicky somehow. Only she's different. Been everywhere you ever heard of, but she wasn't here half an hour before she seemed just like a real Alaskan.'

'Is she pretty?'

Rod nodded as though this could be taken for granted. 'Only you forget about her looks. They don't seem important. Her hair isn't blonde like Vicky's, or even red, but something in between. Kind of bronze with a lot of gold in it. And her eyes are sort of grey and brown, and when she laughs, there are funny tints in them.'

Spence smiled. For a girl whose looks were unimportant, this was a fairly comprehensive description. 'Are they going to buy supplies from you?'

'Yes. They didn't know they could get fresh meat and vegetables nearer than Juneau, but I told them you could make Shaman Cove your first call and—'

'I can't this week. The Seal Point saltery is in a hurry for a shipment, but I'll—'

'Oh, that's all right,' Rod said. 'I'll run it down tomorrow morning.'

'Sure you can spare the time?' Spence asked dryly.

'I have to go anyway.' If Spence was trying to be funny, it was better to ignore it. 'I've got to see the cook and find out what he'd like to have me save for him on boat days. And Judy—that's her name—is making a list of things she needs for a new cabin. Paint, and curtains—stuff like that.'

'Then you can tell them I'll stop in when I'm back from Seal Point.'

Rod nodded. 'But that isn't the reason I brought you in here.' He paused a moment, and his eyes avoided the other's. 'Wanted to tell you if you find me gone in the next week or so, don't ask questions. I'm telling people I have to go to Juneau.'

'Who's taking care of the store?'

'Henry Dane.' Then as Spence looked at him in surprise, he added quickly, 'He'll do all right.'

'He never did when he ran the store!'

'Henry's different now. He's fed up with doing nothing but fussing with the little mail that Rampart gets, and he'd like to be a clerk. And I might need one.' He flushed under

41

Rod eased his motor boat up to the new log float in Shaman Cove. He didn't see anyone in the mining camp on the bench above, but before he'd made fast, Judy came running down the steps cut into the steep bank. He gave her the mail sack and began to unload the groceries.

'Spence couldn't get here for a few days, and I was afraid the fresh vegetables might spoil. Especially the tomatoes.'

'Tomatoes!' she exclaimed. 'I want to watch Sang's face when he sees them!'

'That's easy. We'll carry them up in the first load.'

'And he can help you with the rest. I'd call him except he never understands me. Or pretends he doesn't. But now I'll have a chance to see that sign language of yours in action.'

They arrived at the cook camp bearing booty. Sang's applause was overwhelming, first in voluble Chinese, then in signs, and finally, when the meat was brought and he explained future orders should have larger roasts and more steak, he was using plain English.

'I thought he understood more than he let you know,' Rod said as they left the cook camp.

'But why?'

'A good Chinese cook doesn't believe in women around a kitchen.'

'And what does he expect me to do?'

'Sit around and be beautiful.' Rod's smile suggested she'd find this very easy. 'You're the boss's daughter.'

'I'm glad Alec doesn't feel that way about it. He and Father will be here soon. They must have seen your boat. You'll stay for lunch, won't you?'

'I hoped you'd ask me.'

'Then you can stay! That's wonderful! And I want to show you the plans for our new cabin.'

She spread them out on her father's desk.

'We'll keep this office as his workshop, with a door leading to the living-room beyond—a big room with a lot of windows looking out across the bay at that mountain and the river. We won't need pictures with a view like that. My bedroom is at the end of the wing we are adding. And Alec says I can have all the shelves and built-in chests I want. I've never had enough.'

Rod studied the drawings. 'Looks like quite a house,' he said.

'Isn't it? We put in the stakes last evening. Come and see the view I'll wake up to every morning.' He followed her outside. 'Look at that! The mountain valley, and all the peaks beyond! Isn't it—well—simply stupendous!' She laughed apologetically. 'It's a big word, but you have to use them when you talk about this country. And the colours! You can't believe them!'

He looked at her, face alight and eyes shining. 'You must like Alaska.'

'Like! I'm crazy about it! I have been ever since our trip from Juneau. And every day it seems more wonderful. I'm still finding new shades and tints I'd missed before. That's why it's been so hard to choose the colours for the paints. You see—I want to bring Alaska indoors. Or does that sound too ambitious?'

It did, but he didn't like to say so. He'd never met a girl who talked like this, but he found her ideas intriguing. 'It's a sort of large order,' he said at last. 'What colour did you decide on?'

'I'm going to stain the walls—a warm tint, not too dark, just enough to take the rawness off new lumber and make a backdrop for all those exciting greens and greys and rose shades of the lichens. Of course I'll need some spots of vivid colour. And I found exactly the right thing for upholstery, a sort of green or blue, whichever you want to call it. Like the spruce forest on that mountain. Don't you think that will be good?'

He looked at the mantled slope. 'Spruces are a bluish green. I never thought of it before.'

'With a silver sheen,' she said. 'But you're so used to it,

45

you didn't notice. In my room I'm going to have clear lemon yellow curtains and paint the walls. I want that soft blue, almost smoky, but with a warm cast—the colour of far-off mountain peaks. There's nothing like it on the card, but one of the men used to be a painter, and he promised to help me mix it.'

Rod was beginning to feel lost, especially as she so evidently expected him to have convictions. He knew he liked some colours better than others, and he'd approved of what Vicky had done in her studio at Hidden Harbour, but paints came out of cans and weren't mixed up to match a mountain. Yet, if a girl as nice as Judy could get so stirred up over a particular shade, he'd like to share her excitement. Vicky would have understood, and so would Phil, and he was wishing that he did when, to his relief, Mr Randolph and another man joined them. Judy introduced Alec.

Rod liked him instantly, liked the way he shook hands, and realized why Judy had hesitated about his status. The title, straw boss, wasn't big enough for a person like Alec.

'Rod brought the mail sack, Dad,' Judy said. 'It's on your desk.'

'Thank you, Rod.' David Randolph started for the cabin, then turned to say, 'You're staying for lunch, of course.' Rod said he was, and the other nodded. 'Good,' he said. 'I'll see you later.'

'I've been showing Rod how grand our house is going to be,' Judy explained.

'Better not do too much crowing until I've had a chance to find out how much lumber we've got around here,' Alec said.

'You can get anything you need from the sawmill at Rampart Bay,' Rod said.

'So? I heard about a boat works and a store and cannery, but nobody mentioned any sawmill. How'd we get the stuff down here?'

'Charlie Reynolds has a tug. He's the owner of the mill. And Spence could take your order up when he comes in this week.'

'Fine. I'll figure it out tonight and have it ready for him.

And now would you care to go up and see how we look inside a mountain? There's just time before the crew knocks off for dinner.'

'I'd like to. I've never seen a diamond drill in action.'

As the three climbed the slope, Alec explained some of their problems, then stopped beside a drill. Alec picked up a six-inch piece of core. 'This came out first, from the surface rock,' he said.

Rod examined it carefully. 'I see!' he exclaimed. 'You use a circular bit to cut this, and then it's lifted out. Why, if you run into quartz, you know exactly what it is and where it's lying.'

'That's the idea,' Alec said.

They climbed to another drill and looked at more cores. Rod found the accuracy of their knowledge fascinating. Before they were through, they'd know the secrets of that mountain. He was disappointed when Alec looked at his watch and said it was dinnertime. Rod nodded and walked to where a workman was fitting the last core to the others in a long wooden frame. 'Just a minute,' he called.

Alec grinned. 'Smart kid,' he said to Judy. 'Let's you and me get started. They'll come along when they're ready.'

As she and Alec followed the trail down the slope, she wondered about Alec's comment. Mr Daniels had said Rod was smart but that this was his trouble. Apparently Alec didn't feel so.

'Why did you say Rod was smart?' she asked.

'Because he don't ask any questions his own head can answer.'

She considered this for a moment. 'Perhaps it's only because he's too proud to ask them. I know I am.'

'Pride ain't a bad fault, is it? I can think of others a whole lot worse.'

The crew and Rod caught up with them, and they all trooped in to the cook camp together. The aroma of sizzling steak was in the air, and Sang was beaming. As he led Rod to his place at the head of the table with the Randolphs and Alec, he left no doubt in anyone's mind who was responsible for the booty.

47

Afterwards when the men had gone back to work Rod said how much he liked Alec.

'And he likes you,' Judy said. 'I noticed he talked to you all during lunch.'

'He was only asking me how I happened to start a trollers' store.'

'I heard you telling him about it.'

'There wasn't much to tell. It was a natural with a bunch of trollers on the strait who wanted to tie up nights where they could buy the stuff they needed at decent prices and get together without being made to feel anyone was doing them a favour. A lot of them are bachelors, and Rampart is their only home port. They're fine fellows and hard workers too. They're off before daybreak, and when kings are running right, they don't stop till dark. It's only when the weather's rough they get in early enough for a game of pinochle in the evening.'

'I'd wondered why you had a card table and benches,' she said. 'Why—it's like a club! Did you always want a store?'

'Not especially.' Then after a moment he went on. 'When I was a kid and Spence was always talking about how we ought to get out of Hidden Harbour and move to some place on the coast, I used to think he and I would build a town and call it Baird. I don't remember how I planned we'd start it. A kid of twelve doesn't worry about such things. He just dreams. Even later, that summer I worked at the cannery, I didn't especially want a store. Maybe I never would have had one, if Spence hadn't owned the float and house and Henry Dane hadn't made such a mess of storekeeping.'

'But it's more than just a store! It's a town, really. You feel that, in the way you talk about it.'

'Think so?' He was surprised at how much her speech had pleased him. Of course she didn't know about those first months and what the friendship of the trollers and Charlie Reynolds had really meant. Nor how he needed it. And there was no use in trying to tell her. 'It's sort of a little town, in a way,' he said. 'Later, when the kings are

48

really running on the strait and the whole gang is back you ought to come in some evening and see it going full blast.'

'I will, if I'm still here,' she said

'Thought you were going to stay all summer!'

'I said I hoped I could.' She paused. 'But that depends on—oh—a lot of things—Father—and how he feels about my staying in Alaska. It isn't that he doesn't like to have me here,' she added quickly. 'I know that. It's only because he worries—about—about his duty as a parent. You know how men are about the things they don't quite understand. But anyway I'll be here until the cabin is finished. And he's as pleased as I am.' She seemed very anxious that Rod believe this. 'Then afterwards—'

'You'll have to stay long enough to enjoy all that fancy painting,' he said quickly. He saw she didn't want to talk about it. Usually she was so definite about everything. 'Is your list of the things you want me to order for you ready?'

'But you told Dad that Spence would be in to pick up the mail for next boat day!'

'And he will. Only I want to be sure this order gets off, and I might not be in Rampart when the *Taku* comes in.' He paused. 'You see,' he said, 'I've got to go on a trip.'

'Oh! Will you be gone long?'

'Not very. Perhaps a week. Maybe ten days.'

He didn't like to make a mystery about it, but somehow he couldn't tell her that yarn about having to go to Juneau. He hoped she wouldn't ask any questions, but when she didn't, he found this equally unsatisfactory.

'You see,' he went on after a long silence. 'It's something I've been planning for a long time. I'm not going very far—only to a camp on Admiralty, but I don't know how long I'll have to be away. I'll tell you about it sometime. But—right now—well, I promised somebody I wouldn't talk about it.' That was true enough he thought, even if the somebody was himself. 'What do you want to do this afternoon?'

'Do you know this cove?'

He nodded. 'Came in for shelter once when a three-day

south-easter was blowing. There's a nice river up the valley.'

'With a high falls at its mouth. I've seen that.'

'Above the falls the river's fine. Have to wade in places. Better wear hip boots.'

'But I don't own any. The travel agency never even mentioned them. I should have bought them when I was at the store. Why didn't you tell me?'

'I haven't any small enough to fit you. You must wear about Vicky's size, and hers were a special order. Put boots on that list of yours. Until you've gone up rivers, you haven't seen Alaska. But I know what we can do! There's a fine crab flat across the bay where that little stream comes in. Tide is running out now, and the crabs will be heading for deeper water. I've got a dip net aboard the boat.'

'Did you bring it on purpose?'

'Had an idea it might be fun. We can scoop them off the bottom.'

Her eyes lighted. 'I'll tell Sang he'll have crabs for supper and meet you at the float.'

When she arrived, the mine skiff was already equipped with net, a gunny sack, and a large wooden box. She asked what it was for.

'These are fighting crabs, and you don't want them crawling around your feet.'

'Do you always think of everything?' she asked.

'Not always.' Then he grinned. 'But you see this is the first time I've ever taken a girl out on a crab hunt.' He'd been tempted to say it was the first time he'd ever taken a girl anywhere, but hadn't quite had the courage.

She laughed. 'And it's the first time anyone at all has invited me to go crabbing.'

'I suppose it is,' he said. As he rowed across the bay, he thought about this. To a girl who'd done the things she must have—who knew theatres and restaurants and parties —a crab hunt must seem a very childish pastime. Yet she appeared to be having a good time.

He was sure of this presently when he lifted their first crab in the net and held it high in the air to her applause and delight. And when a moment later the crab almost managed to escape over the metal ring of the net, she was beside herself with dismay.

'Don't lose him!' she cried. 'Don't you dare lose him! I couldn't bear it!'

He had somewhat the feeling of a triumphant gladiator as he dumped their trophy in the box, where it glared at them with beady eyes and clicked its claws in rage.

'It's the biggest crab I ever saw!' she exclaimed.

'It's not so big. Shell won't run over seven inches.' He peered overside. 'There's a bigger one coming now. Want to try it?'

'Can I?' A second later she was in the bow with the dip net poised.

'Head him off! Quick! Before he gets past you,' Rod shouted as he swung the skiff in the crab's direction.

For a moment he feared she was going overboard in her frantic thrust of the long handle, and then she triumphantly brought net and crab above the surface. In a moment it had joined its fellow in the box.

'It'll run over nine inches easy,' Rod said. 'Let's see if I can beat it. Tell you what! We'll take turns and keep score. Biggest crab of a pair gets you one point. A miss loses two points, and anything under the legal limit goes back into the water and costs a penalty of three. So far you're a point ahead.'

They pursued crabs industriously, argued amiably about comparative sizes, and made new rules to cover penalties. Judy pointed out that a miss should be called so only if the lost crab had been definitely within net reach, and that her arms were shorter than his. He conceded this, and they gravely measured net reach, and established a six-inch handicap. This ruling brought her score gratifyingly near his.

At last Rod counted their catch. 'Fifteen,' he said. 'Can the crew eat more than that?'

'Not even this many.' She reluctantly laid down the net. 'Would you believe fifteen crabs could make all that racket?'

The clicking claws were now an angry chorus. Rod dipped a sack in water and covered them tightly. 'Maybe this will keep them quiet.' It didn't, but it subdued the chatter somewhat. 'Let's go ashore and look around,' he said. 'I don't have to start home for another hour, and there's plenty of time for Sang to cook the crabs for supper.'

'How do you cook crabs like these?' she asked.

'Vicky always did it Tlingit fashion. Boiled them in sea water and we ate them hot, but—'

'We'll let Sang decide how he wants to do it,' she finished for him. 'Only sometime I'd like to try the Tlingit way.'

'Sure. We'll take along a big kettle and have a crab feed on a beach.'

She nodded as though it were only natural they'd do many things together, and as he rowed ashore, he wished she knew more about him. That first day when he'd told her he had worked on a purse seiner, he'd never meant to claim he'd been a real hand on a fishing boat. But it had sounded that way, and she'd have every reason to believe it did. She was so frank and outright, it would never occur to her he could have meant anything else.

He looked at her in the stern, laughing and talking about their crab hunt. They were like old friends who'd had a good time together. You didn't let down a girl like Judy by having her find out things about you later. Maybe she never would, but anyway you couldn't feel right about it. You'd want to tell her yourself.

He drew the skiff up on the flat and carried a long line to the higher ground, where he made it fast. 'We can't go far away,' he said. 'When the tide turns, I'll have to pull the line in.'

'I don't want to go any farther. This is lovely.'

The little stream wound through a sunlit gash between steep granite shoulders. Waist-high ferns, bleeding hearts, and white asters adorned the banks, swaying in the breeze above the sparkling water. Judy found a grassy hummock, sat down, and settled back against a tree trunk. She looked up the mountain.

'I suppose, way, way back there, this little brook is only a waterfall that leapt off a mountain and started for the sea.' She smiled at him. 'When I get my hip boots, we can go exploring.'

He nodded. There was so much they could do together,

and then he remembered. Perhaps she wouldn't want to. His face sobered.

'What's the matter?' she asked. 'Or don't you like exploring? Don't tell me you hate it as much as fishing.'

'That wasn't fishing,' he said harshly. She looked at him puzzled. 'Aboard the purse seiner, I mean. And when I told you, I never intended to claim I'd been a real purse seiner.'

'Oh! And that's why Mr Daniels asked me if you were on the *Sea Lion*!'

'He did!' Rod exclaimed. 'Then he must have had a hunch, but it doesn't matter now. It's a long story, but I'd like you to know it—if you don't mind listening to—' He broke off and gathered a handful of gravel and tossed it, pebble by pebble, into the stream, watching each fall with a little plop. Then he turned to face her. 'It would put things square and straight between us.'

She nodded, and he saw from her eyes she understood.

'The story goes a long way back,' he began. 'But don't think I didn't have the finest family any kid ever had. Jeff might have had a few notions about our living off by ourselves, but Spence and Vicky came through all right. Only I didn't fit in somehow. Mostly because I didn't want to. I don't know what I wanted, except to have things different. I was always planning on how I'd get away and do things on my own.'

She laughed. 'I thought every boy dreamed about going west and being a famous scout or mighty hunter.'

'I could have done all that at home! Plenty of empty country around us. My ideas were different. So the first year Daniels took over the cannery, I went to Rampart and got a job as timekeeper and store clerk. And was I set up about it! The fellow who had the job before me was a man, full grown, and I'd had to lie about my age to make Daniels take me. And now I had my chance to prove I could get somewhere in the world, and on my own. Had a new idea every minute.

'Some of them weren't so good, but a few had sense to them. You see in a little place like Rampart you've got to pull together. Daniels expected Charlie Reynolds to sell him

'When it was dark, we ran the *Sea Lion* to the trap, but we didn't know Daniels had armed his watchmen. We were tied up and Frank was out on the trap timbers when the watchman started shooting. He got Frank through the head. I saw him drop. The second bullet clipped me in the leg. I was in the wheelhouse. Pete ran out to bring in the lines and pull out of range. We were expecting a lot more bullets. Afterwards I heard that the gun had jammed. But right then, if I could have walked, I'd have climbed off the *Sea Lion* and let the watchman catch me. I hadn't counted on any shooting. Frank was dead. Pete was mean and ugly and as scared as I was. I don't know what would have happened to me.

'Then all of a sudden I heard the *Taku's* motor, and in another minute Spence came aboard and made Pete help him carry me to the *Taku*. That's the kind of a brother Spence is! He'd heard the shooting, guessed what was going on, and he and Chris had switched off the *Taku's* lights and run in to get me.'

'Not Chris Daniels!'

'Sure. She'd come up here on Richards' yacht to visit her father.'

'Go on,' Judy said tensely. 'This—this is— What happened then?'

'Nothing much. Chris bandaged my leg and took care of ₁ne while Spence ran the *Taku* to the Tlingit village in Falcon Inlet. He couldn't keep me on his boat at Rampart with everybody talking about the shooting, and if he took me home, Jeff and Mom would know what I'd been doing. So they took me to some Tlingit friends of Spence's—an old carver and his wife. I lived with Sha-goon-e-ish and Jennie for two months, until I could walk again.'

'Didn't Chris ever tell her father?'

'Of course she didn't. That was only a hunch he had, and it doesn't matter anyway. I never took a fish from his traps. Nor any other canner's since then.'

'And your family? Didn't they find out?'

'Not Mom or Vicky. Jeff did. Next morning he saw the *Taku* at the village, found blood on the deck, and came up to the house where Sha-goon-e-ish lived. I'll never forget seeing Jeff walk in the door.'

'What—' she began. 'Oh, I shouldn't have—'

'I want to tell you.' His voice was proud. 'All he said was that for a Baird I was awful slow in growing up.'

There was a long moment of silence. Rod stared at the stream. He wasn't sure she'd understood just what he had been trying to tell her or even what a grand person Jeff really was. She'd probably heard a lot of stuff from Daniels about how Jeff tried to keep his family off at the head of Falcon Inlet.

'Afterwards Jeff used to come and visit me,' he went on. 'I got to know him better than I ever had before. That's one thing those two months did.' He stopped, then realized she was waiting for him to finish. 'But it isn't all they did. I decided if I was one tenth as smart as I'd thought I was, I'd better start to prove it, even if only to myself.' He stood up. 'I warned you it was a long story. I've never told it to anyone before—not even Vicky.'

'But I'm so glad you did tell me, Rod. It was—it was—it shows you trust me.'

For two years he and Sha-goon-e-ish had made furtive trips across the strait to Tallac Bay on Admiralty. Rod knew he couldn't afford the dynamite or the old carver's wages, but he spent the money anyhow. They deepened channels, blew out barricades, and Sha-goon-e-ish had camped on the river to count spawners. The first summer there had been only a thin dribble going up the river. The second there had been more.

Now the spawn of that first thin dribble were two years old and should be coming back. Might already have come if the seine boat had made its haul close to Rampart Bay. He had to know where those pinks had been caught.

A few moments later he was in his motor boat and on his way to the cannery. When he reached the wharf, the jubilant skipper was still telling his story to anyone who had time to listen.

'First boat to bring in pinks!' he exulted. 'More'n ten thousand! Got 'em way down the channel off Bear Point.'

Rod looked into the hold of the seiner. The silvery fish reached almost deck-high. Gleaming, all the same size—there were the two-year-olds that had been bound for home stream. And in this compelling urge, they would fill fish traps and holds of vessels, yet enough would reach their goal to insure survival of the species.

Back at the store Rod hurried to Henry Dane's small cabin. Henry came to the door in answer to Rod's knock.

'I've got to go to Juneau,' Rod said.

'Made up your mind in a hurry. Get a wire at the cannery?'

'It didn't come. That's why I'm going. Have to straighten out this account or I'll have trouble all summer.'

'Don't I know!' Henry nodded. 'Wholesalers! Bah! Write you letters and don't even read the—'

'I'll be here this evening to take care of trollers and tell them you're the boss while I'm away.' Henry's eyes flickered in anticipation. 'And I'll write out orders for the next shipment so you won't—'

'Don't you worry,' Henry said. 'Remember I ran this store before you got here.'

'Sure you did! One boat day isn't going to bother you, and I'll be back before the next one.'

Rod worked late that night and was grateful for the need to do so. It kept him from thinking too much about what he'd find at Tallac tomorrow. Next morning he departed long before daylight. As he left, he saw lights in several trolling boats, but he'd be well across the strait before their skippers were out fishing. And soon the need of all this secrecy would be over. Once the Bairds had their licences for trap sites, he wouldn't care if the whole world knew it.

He dropped anchor off the mouth of the river, went ashore, and hurried up the trail to the old Indian encampment. The ancient clearing was overgrown with brush and trees, but Sha-goon-e-ish had reclaimed a spot near the river-bank. Jennie sat in the doorway of their cedar-matting hut, weaving a basket. Her wrinkled parchment-like face broke into smiles.

Rod put down a sack of groceries. 'There's more on the beach,' he said. 'Sha-goon-e-ish and I'll get it later. Where is he?'

She said he was at the counting place, a narrow stretch where swimming fish could easily be seen. As Rod walked upriver, he watched the riffles ahead and stopped to study the pools beneath the cut banks. There were no fish in sight. Sha-goon-e-ish saw him coming and shook his head.

'None at all?' Rod asked.

Sha-goon-e-ish shrugged. 'Ten or twelve, maybe. That's all.'

They might be the leaders or they might be only the same old dribble of pink salmon Rod had watched two years before. Still, it was only yesterday that the purse seiner had made his haul far down the strait, and the pinks had a long way to come.

'Couldn't expect them for a few days,' Rod said with a confidence he didn't feel.

Sha-goon-e-ish went on staring at the river. Rod wished he had the Indian's patience to sit and wait, but he was too wrought up, too restless, and while anything he did now might prove to be wasted work, at least he'd be doing something. He returned to the beach and made a rough chart of the bay. Fishing regulations did not permit a trap within five hundred yards of the mouth of a salmon river or within six hundred yards of another trap. Rod paced off five hundred yards on each side, marked the spots on his chart, then paced the distance to the outer points of the bay. It was slow and heavy going, even at half tide. In many places the rocky shores rose sheer from the water, and it was suppertime before he'd finished.

Jennie had constructed a separate cedar-matting shelter for Rod and prepared a meal. He was glad it was venison stew, and no one spoke of Tallac pinks.

Next morning Sha-goon-e-ish departed for the counting place, and Rod returned to the bay to study currents in the high spring tide. These would not only influence the route fish would follow but would determine the weight of the trap's anchor gear. By throwing a small block of wood overboard, taking a sight ashore, and watching the block's speed and direction, he charted the currents in various stages of the tides inside the bay and out beyond the points where the pinks would turn to the home stream.

The next day he finished prospecting the two trap sites. He took sounds to discover the necessary length of the anchor cables and rechecked the distance to the north and south outer points of the bay. He was jubilant. By placing one trap on the north side and the other on the south shore, both beyond the required five hundred yards from the river mouth, no one else could obtain a licence on either shore without being within six hundred yards of a Baird trap.

He marked the sites, blazed a tree above each, and wrote 'Baird' on the exposed wood. In his mind he was already composing the application. 'North shore beneath a blazed hemlock, seven hundred yards from Grief Point. On the south side beneath a blazed cedar, six hundred yards from the river mouth and four hundred yards from the rock at the entrance.'

At supper Sha-goon-e-ish reported thirty pinks had gone up stream. Jennie looked at Rod and uttered clucking noises of sympathy. He smiled at her. With a bay so miraculously proportioned for only two trap sites he couldn't feel downhearted.

Next morning Rod went back to the counting place with Sha-goon-e-ish. The old carver clicked his meter several times, but the clicks had a mournful sound. There were even fewer fish than the day before. It was only the same old dribble, and Sha-goon-e-ish, who had been watching for a week, made no effort to conceal his hopelessness. When Rod could endure it no longer, he went back to camp. His thoughts were bitter as he stared into Jennie's cooking fire.

He should have known that if the idea was any good, someone would have done it long ago. With every canner on the coast striving for a larger pack each season, exploring for new trap sites, fighting to get salmon, why had he ever dreamed he could find a way to bring back a river or put his hopes on so simple an answer as clearing out a stream?

Jennie brought him a plate of food. He thanked her and set it down without making even a pretence of eating. Jennie shook her head sorrowfully and went back to sit beside the river. He was still thinking of the two years he had wasted when he heard her soft ejaculation.

'Pst! Pst!' she said and pointed. 'The salmon!' and only one of a race who had lived for centuries on its bounty could have put so much feeling into the words.

Rod leaped to his feet. A steady stream of fish was swimming up the channel, sometimes two or three abreast, and as the leaders passed him, he could see more coming below. Rod stared a moment, then ran for the counting place.

Sha-goon-e-ish's broad face was wreathed in smiles as he clicked the meter in quick succession. Another lot followed, then another and another. The main run had started. Rod was sure of it by evening when the old carver held up the meter.

'No good,' he said. 'One click—ten fish.'

Now the water above the shallows was white with fins and thrashing tails. Rod grabbed the meter and tried to keep count, but it was useless. They could only estimate the number.

All the next day and the following, Rod counted and estimated. He made himself remain to be certain this was no small remnant arriving in a body. But all the time he was thinking of the trap sites and the need to get the licences before anyone could possibly discover the Tallac pinks were coming back. And thinking too of what those traps would mean to the others. Mom, not having to work so hard and scrimp; Jeff, free to roam his beloved country and choose only the trees that were a challenge, instead of always driving to get logs to the sawmill; Spence, with a line of coastwise boats and not compelled to take every small towing job that came his way. These were things he could put into words. The other—what it might mean to have accomplished something, to have restored a salmon stream that would multiply its riches through the years—this he didn't let himself even think about.

As Rod turned into Rampart Bay, he was hoping Henry Dane knew Spence's schedule on the freight run. Then he saw the *Taku* at the float.

'Where've you been?' Spence called out of the wheelhouse as Rod made fast. 'Phil sent a cable. Jefferson Baird Trent arrived. Phil says he looks like Jeff. And you should have seen Jeff's face when he read that!'

'How's Vicky?' Rod asked.

'Fine! I hate to think what that long cable cost Phil, but he said there'd be another in a few days. I stuck around in case the cannery boat brought it today from Juneau. Promised I'd take the message to Hidden Harbour the minute it got in.'

'Now I'm here, and I can take it to them,' Rod said as he went aboard the *Taku*. 'Need to see Jeff anyway.'

Spence glanced at him sharply but asked no questions. Instead he gave the news from Shaman Cove. He'd called in twice and liked the Randolphs. 'You're right about Judy,' he said. 'She's a peach!'

'Think so?' Rod tried to sound non-committal. 'Did Charlie Reynolds take their lumber to them?'

Spence nodded. 'Last time I was in, Alec had almost

finished the house. Judy asked when you'd be back, but I told her you'd had more to do in Juneau than you'd expected.'

'You did!' Rod exclaimed, and then remembered Spence had said only what he'd been told to say. He couldn't blame Spence, but Judy must have thought it was sort of queer.

'Trip go all right, kid?' Spence asked.

Rod gulped. 'Fine,' he said. 'And you're going to get a licence for a fish trap in Tallac Bay.'

'Tallac! Are you crazy! The Indians fished that stream out years ago. Haven't been enough pinks to make it even worth *their* while.'

'There are now.'

'And what would I do with a licence for a trap site?'

'You'll have to get one, Spence. You're over twenty-one and can get it. Jeff can get the other. Listen while I tell you.' He glanced out the wheelhouse door. 'Let's go below. We've got to keep this on the quiet and do it in a hurry.'

Spence led the way, threw some gear off the transom berth, motioned Rod to sit down, and sat beside him. 'Go ahead. I'm listening. At first I thought you were joking.'

Rod told the story. He started at the beginning and tried to tell it quietly. He didn't want Spence to think this was just a kid's wild idea.

'Does anybody except Sha-goon-e-ish and Jennie know about this?' Spence asked at last.

'Only Vicky. I had to tell her where I was going that time I asked her to tend the store. Besides I wanted to. I couldn't keep it to myself much longer.'

'Who could?' Spence said. 'An idea like that! Two years! I got to hand it to you, kid.' His face was working strangely, and then he laughed. 'And when Vicky told me you had gone to Point Alexander to start a store there, I believed her! Thought all you wanted to do was sell canned stuff to trollers.'

'She knew it wasn't that way with me,' Rod said. 'She was all for this. And she's got a share in the traps coming.

So has Sha-goon-e-ish. But we can figure all that out after you and Jeff get the site licences.'

'Sure,' Spence said. 'But why do you think the run will be bigger next year?'

'It's this way. In '12 we cleaned out the river and counted spawners. There was only a dribble. In '13 we did some more work and counted them again. The '13 run was bigger than in '12. At least twice as many. I don't know why. I wish I could figure why one run should be so much better.'

'So would a lot of canners. But no one's done it yet.'

'Well, anyway,' Rod went on. 'The spawn from the '12 dribble are back now in '14. It's a fair run. Nothing you'd build traps for. But if a dribble could seed the river that well, the '13 run, twice as big, will do a whole lot better. So the run in '15 is bound to be a good one.'

Spence nodded. 'That makes sense.'

'And we'd be set, own the sites, have the traps built— all ready for the big run two years from now when the spawn from this summer comes back. That's the run I'm looking for!' His voice cracked a little as he said, 'Why— why—we might get over half a million fish!'

Spence's eyes gleamed. 'At the price canneries are paying now that would run into'—he stopped to calculate—'over thirty thousand dollars! In one season!'

'Sure,' Rod said.

For a moment Spence looked at the other incredulously, and then as suddenly as he had caught fire he came swiftly down to earth.

'You and me! Sitting here talking about building floating traps! We must be crazy. Where'd we ever get that kind of money?'

'But they wouldn't cost us anywhere near what they'd cost a cannery. Jeff can log the timbers, like he did for Daniels, and these aren't outside traps in deep water. We'd be sheltered, won't need heavy gear nor as many anchors or anywhere near as much steel cable.'

'Still have to buy it. And hire a crew to build and rig them. Ever figure what even an inside trap can run to?'

'What do you think I've been doing while I was in Tallac?

I took soundings and studied currents. It's all written down in the chart. I can show it to you. And we wouldn't have to hire a big crew. We could do a lot of the work ourselves. Plenty of ways we could save money.'

'Steel cable, webbing, and the gear would run into mo than six thousand dollars.'

'But we can borrow that from the cannery.'

Spence frowned. Rod thought he was like Jeff in hating to owe anybody.

'Independent owners always have to borrow! You know that, Spence. They couldn't build a trap unless a cannery backed them. And any canner is glad to do it. All he wants is fish to pack. Daniels knows there aren't any more good trap sites left around here. He'd jump at the chance to get the Tallac pinks.'

'We'd be getting in awful deep,' Spence said thoughtfully.

'Not for long! We could pay it off the first season. Be in the clear for the big run in '16.'

Spence nodded. 'I suppose we could be by that time,' he said, and then he smiled. 'I guess it was the idea of us borrowing that kind of money. But it wouldn't mean anything to Daniels.'

'And it's our chance! A chance for all of us! Those Tallac pinks are Baird salmon, if fish ever belonged to anybody.'

'You sure earned them, kid. Two years! It's a long time to wait to find out if you've guessed right. And I bet no one else ever stopped to wonder why the Tallac run had dwindled out!'

'Maybe I wouldn't have if—if things had been different with me,' Rod said, and then he shrugged. 'We ought to get those licences in a hurry. I've got the applications in my boat. I'll get them and the chart I made of the bay.'

He was back in a moment with the packet. 'Last winter I wrote to Juneau for the fishing laws. Thought they might come in handy.'

Spence, already studying Rod's chart of the bay, looked up and laughed. 'They sure did,' he said. 'The way you've spotted these traps, no one can cut us off on either side.'

He read through the laws and whistled when he saw the two-hundred-dollar licence fee. 'Never knew it was that much! And another tax if a trap catches more than 100,000 fish a season! That we wouldn't mind paying, and all we have to dig up now are licence fees. I'll take care of them.'

'You pay yours. Besides, you have to make the trip to Juneau to get the licences. But I'll pay Jeff's fee. Planned on doing it, and we ought to ask him which trap he wants.'

'You sure he'll want one?' Spence asked quickly, and when Rod didn't answer, he added, 'And what makes you sure?'

'Jeff has changed a lot since Vicky went off to New York. You know that, Spence. Remember how Mom was always asking him to let her help him learn to read? Well, now he's learned. First it was on account of Vicky's letter, but now you ought to see him grab for the magazines and papers. He used to think all they were good for was to build a fire. And even long before that when—'

He didn't finish, but of course Spence knew he was thinking of those months in the Tlingit village and how Jeff had made special trips to see him and hadn't been half as stirred up about his running away or even the shooting as Spence was. Jeff had only said he'd never had a chance to cut his own trails the way any real Baird had to.

'Jeff understands a lot of things we never thought he did when we were kids in Hidden Harbour,' Rod said at last. 'I know that now.'

'He still feels the same about salmon and the tourists. You've heard him!'

Rod nodded. He knew the speeches that had always bothered Spence. Now salmon and the tourists were nothing a man could count on; here today and gone tomorrow. But trees held a future. A man knew they would be there waiting for him to come and get them, and he knew another forest would grow up for his children. Jeff had said this often. And now Rod had a strange conviction that Jeff would understand about Tallac River and what it could mean. A man who had nursed a mountainside of trees, foreseeing the need of forests in the future, and who had gloried in the richness of a country was bound to understand and want to be a part of the venture. Yet he couldn't have explained this.

'I don't know how he feels,' Rod said, 'but he has a right to be asked about it. This—this—it's not just you and me, Spence. It's a Baird affair.'

6

It was almost noon when Rod rounded the point of Hidden Harbour and blew his whistle. He had waited for Phil's second cable, and now when his mother ran down the path to meet him, he waved the yellow envelope. It was the best present he could bring her.

She caught the bow line and made it fast. 'It's good to see you, Rod!' she said and reached up to pat his shoulder when he kissed her.

Rod laughed indulgently. She always seemed so small. Her head barely reached his chin, but there was nothing helpless about her spirit. He handed her the cable, and she smiled as she read the long message.

'Isn't it wonderful of Phil to wire us even the little things—Vicky being so happy to be home again, and the baby already screaming for his meals? Jeff will like that.'

'Where is he?'

'Towing a big spruce home. He's been working on that tree ever since he heard about young Jeff.'

'I didn't see him in the inlet. I'll run back and give him a lift. It's slow work rowing one of those big sticks home.'

'I think he'd rather you wouldn't.' Rod looked at her in surprise. 'He'll want to bring this by himself. It's a very special spruce.' She laughed happily. 'You know the big one in Indian Cove—the one he was afraid would be a hang-up? He figured out a way to fall it, but he'll tell you about it when he gets here.'

They went up the path to the log house, which sprawled along the crest of a slope. The big main room, which served as kitchen and living quarters, was cool despite the cooking stove in the corner. Mary Baird brought a pitcher of wild raspberry shrub and a plate of cookies.

'Jeff may be late for dinner, but don't spoil your appetite. I made a pie this morning. When did you come back from Juneau?'

'I got into Rampart yesterday,' he said.

'And heard about young Jeff!'

He nodded. 'And was I glad! Don't think you and Jeff could have waited much longer. How's it seem to be a grandmother?'

'Wonderful!' And the words sang. 'I didn't know how wonderful until it actually happened. And you'd think Jeff was the first man in the world to have a grandson. To hear him talk, the baby is all Baird. No Spencer, no Trent—no ancestors at all except the Bairds. But I'm glad he feels that way, and Vicky will be too.'

Rod laughed and went over to look at Vicky's picture. He'd often wondered why Judy reminded him of her, and now he could see no resemblance in the features. Yet there was the same look about them.

'Surely you must have seen that picture before,' his mother said. 'Mr Streeter sent it to us. I like it better than any Phil has taken.'

'I was only wondering how come she looks so much like a girl who's living in Shaman Cove.'

'Really!'

'She's David Randolph's daughter. Her name is Judy. Randolph's opening up a mine, or thinking about it anyway. I don't know what it is about her that makes me think of Vicky, unless it's only a way they have—as though they were looking off at high mountains and expecting something wonderful to happen.'

'I know that look! She must be nice!'

'She is! I don't know her very well. She and her father were in the store, and then when I took some stuff to their camp, they asked me to stay for lunch. You'd like them, Mom.'

He went on to tell her more about them. His mother was always interested in people, and he told her about the mining camp, the new house they were planning, Judy's vacations, her aunt in Boston, the schools she's gone to, her winter in Paris, and the summer she and her Aunt Nina had travelled through Europe. He was amazed at how much he knew about her.

71

'I guess she's been about everywhere except Alaska, until now,' he said.

'I'd love to meet her. Can't you bring her up to see us?'

'I'd thought of it. Only by the time I went to Shaman Cove to get her and brought her up here, she wouldn't have much of a visit because we'd have to be starting back. But you'll see her sometime in Rampart. She's going to learn how to run their motor boat, and she'd better. It's a cinch her father never can.'

'Then she won't feel so shut in. And here's Jeff now, just coming around the point.'

He was towing the new log. He waved his hat in triumph.

'He'll want us to go down to meet him!' his mother said. 'And remember, Rod, this spruce is really special.'

Jeff always came home a victor when he'd solved a logging problem, but Rod had never known his mother to make such a point of applause before. He understood it better as they watched Jeff open the boom sticks to usher the new log into the little cove among its fellows. The spruce was truly magnificent. Eight feet thick at the butt and three feet across the top, and it must be, Rod estimated, at least 140 feet long. He could only marvel that one man had the skill and cunning to hurl that great mass out and down a mountain.

'That took doing, Jeff,' he said, and there was admiration in his eyes.

'Hah! It was easy, once I had a real reason for figuring how to angle it just right to miss the bench below. Never stopped running. Take a look at the butt. Did you see the mark?' He pointed at the two-foot-high letters, cut in deeply with an axe. ' "J B T." Know who that's for? And from now on young Jeff is going to have one good stick in every batch of logs I send to market. You tell Phil and Vicky next time you write 'em, Mary.'

'Young Jeff will never get a bigger tree,' Rod said.

' 'Fraid not, but he'll get good ones. This'—and Jeff's glance travelled down its length—'has enough lumber in it to build five good-sized town houses. You tell 'em that too, Mary. They'll understand. Dinner ready?'

'And waiting for you. I'll run up and set the table.'

Rod remained to help his father shove the spruce behind the boom sticks. Rod was surprised to see how many logs there were bobbing serenely behind the barrier. Jeff was a worker.

'About time I was sending these to market,' Jeff said as they went to the house. 'Prices up now, and I can't keep the young feller waiting too long for his money.' He stopped at the path leading to the kitchen door. 'I'll wash up in the back entry.'

Mary Baird had dinner on the table when Jeff appeared in a fresh shirt and clean khaki pants. As he came in, Rod suddenly wondered how old Jeff really was. He'd never thought of this before. One didn't think of age in Jeff. There was something in the vigour of that erect, deep-chested figure that seemed timeless.

Mary had put Phil's cable beside Jeff's plate, and he chuckled as he read it. 'Screaming for his meals! That's a Baird for you! If a Baird don't like something, he won't stand for it.' He turned to Rod and asked when he got back from Juneau.

'I didn't go to Juneau. Never intended to, but I didn't want anyone to know where I really had gone.' Jeff looked up alertly. 'Did you ever hear that Tallac River used to be one of the finest salmon streams on this coast?'

Jeff grunted. 'Not that I remember of.'

'Sha-goon-e-ish told me about it two years ago.' And from the quick gleam in Jeff's eyes Rod knew his father remembered those months in the Tlingit village. 'People said it was fished out, but I knew there had to be some other reason. Sounds funny, maybe, that I—' He looked at Jeff, begging him to understand. 'Do you remember what you said that time I almost wrecked the *Taku* and ran away?'

'That you'd never had a chance to be right about anything yet?'

'I had chances, same as Spence and Vicky,' Rod broke in quickly. 'But maybe it was on account of what you'd said I got to wondering about the real reason.' He flushed. 'Anyway I went down and had a look.' He told what he had found and how he and Sha-goon-e-ish had cleared the stream and counted spawners. 'I knew I'd have to wait until this summer before I'd have any proof. But I had to try it. Tallac's where I've been this week.'

'Yes.' Jeff leaned forward, his keen eyes suddenly alive. 'And—'

'I was right, Jeff! There's a run of pinks! Not big, but a lot more than you'd expect from those few spawners the summer we first cleared the river. And it shows what—' Rod tried to keep excitement from his voice but he knew he didn't succeed. 'It shows what that river can be some day. Just like old times.'

Mary looked at her husband. 'Two years, Jeff,' she said proudly, 'he's been waiting.'

'And next year there'll be a bigger run,' Rod said. 'Twice as many spawners went up river last summer. There's bound to be!'

'And now you got to figure how you'll get your crop in.' Jeff pushed back his plate. 'Or maybe you done that already.'

Rod nodded. 'It'll take two traps, Jeff. That is, if we cover both sides of the bay, and we'd have to if we're going to build up that river. Of course,' he added quickly, 'if anything happened to the run next year, we'd be—'

'Never was a harvest that didn't have an "if" to it,' Jeff said. 'Isn't that right, Mary?'

'It was that way in Wyoming and before then in Dakota, and I guess everywhere else for that matter. Grain or cattle. Always one thing or another—drought, or early frost, or a snowstorm, or locusts, or some disease nobody ever heard of before.'

Jeff nodded. 'That's the way I always heard it.' He turned to Rod. 'And in '16, when this year's young come back, you'll have a big run.'

'The second crop of two-year-olds!' Rod liked Jeff's way of putting it, for it would be their crop. 'But with two traps in the bay, the Bairds could get it in. Want to see my chart of the cove?' He passed it across the table. 'Had to make it in a hurry, but it will show you the idea.'

Jeff studied the chart, and then he chuckled.

'This sure will bother Daniels. He's so almighty smart hisself, he can't bear to think anyone else has plain common sense. He even told me how to drop a spruce into the salt chuck.'

'And what did you say?' his wife asked.

'I said, "Mister, if you want this job, it's yours. But if it's mine, I don't need no helper for something I been doing ever since you first wore knee britches."'

'Then what happened?' Rod asked. From what he knew of Daniels, there must have been a real explosion.

'Nothing,' Jeff said. 'Except when the job was done, he said he was satisfied, which I knew was his way of saying he was tickled. I'd kept two pile drivers busy. But I never held that spruce against him.' He looked at Rod as a new thought struck him. 'He'll need the fish from those traps, won't he?'

'Never was a canner who got all the fish he wanted.'

'And his last year's pack was light. Richards was sort of burned up about that.' Rod stared at his father. It had always been a mystery how Jeff acquired so much local gossip during his brief visits in Rampart Bay. 'A Tallac run of pinks would come in handy. Did you bring the papers with you?'

Rod produced the applications.

Jeff read them both. 'If it's all the same to Spence, I'll take the south shore.'

'He said to give you the first choice. And we'll figure out the shares for Vicky and Sha-goon-e-ish later.'

'And yours,' Jeff added. 'Too bad your name ain't on one of these, but that's a weak spot you can grow out of.' He wrote 'Jefferson Baird' in careful script, and then he chuckled. 'Four hundred yards from the point on the south entrance of the bay. Why—if you'd built that cove to order, you couldn't have done it better. And now, Mary, how much money we got in the coffee can? Better get it.'

'I'll pay the fee,' Rod said. 'All Spence and I wanted was for you to sign the application.'

Jeff stared at his son. 'I'm a Baird, ain't I?'

Rod flushed. He hadn't meant to hurt Jeff.

Jeff opened the can, counted out the money, laid it on the table. 'And it's about time the Bairds pulled together,' he said.

Rod thrust out his hand, and as he did so, he suddenly realized it was the first time he'd ever done this. Yet he'd always wanted to. 'Thank you,' he said, and then as they gripped firmly, he added, 'Father,' and this too was a first time. 'I knew you'd be with us.' Looking back, he realized he had been sure. It was what he'd been trying to explain to Spence only the day before.

But Jeff had said it so much better.

And it was Jeff who took them both back to comfortable everydayness as Rod, a bit embarrassed, gathered the heap of bills.

'I suppose now we'll have to wait around all summer before those fellows down in Washington even find Tallac River on the map,' Jeff grumbled.

'Spence can get the licences from the fishery bureau in Juneau. He'll have them back here in a week.'

'As easy as that?' asked Jeff, obviously disappointed. He'd been preparing to do battle with a distant and neglectful government.

'We'll own the trap sites before anyone even hears about the run.' It was all so easy, it was almost an anticlimax, and then Rod was suddenly very sober. 'I wish we could be as sure about our crops.'

Jeff nodded, and then the old gleam came to his eyes.

'Son,' he said. 'I couldn't be sure I'd find a country like Hidden Harbour when I loaded you young 'uns and your ma aboard the old *North Star* and sailed off for Alaska. Wasn't even sure I'd get you there. Lot of folks thought I wouldn't.' He filled his pipe and tamped the tobacco slowly, then looked at Rod. 'But it was something I had to do.'

Afterwards on the way home Rod thought about that speech, and never had he felt closer to his father. Jeff's trail had been the search for a country he had seen as in a vision, a land of promise. The dream had been compelling, and its fulfilment had brought deep satisfaction. And now in the restoration of a rich salmon stream, the trails were not so very different. A virgin land, and a desire to preserve its prodigality. A man's compulsion to prove himself and to find pride in an achievement.

Jeff hadn't been thinking only of the hundred of thousands of pink salmon in Baird traps. To him perhaps it hadn't been even the cutting of a new trail but only a fresh turn in the old one, leading to adventure. And no matter what the outcome, it was something a Baird must do.

This was what Jeff had been trying to tell him. And Rod felt much better.

7

AFTER BREAKFAST, when the mine crew had gone to work, Judy went to her father's office.

'Would you like to inspect your house?' she asked.

'I've been hoping I'd be invited. Until now you and Alec have been acting like conspirators.'

'And you've been awfully good about not snooping.' He'd even kept the door of his office closed. 'Sang has just swept up the sawdust.'

She led him in by the new entrance to the main room. Her father looked across at the stretch of windows giving out on the bay and the mountains that flanked it.

'This—this is great, Judy!' he exclaimed. 'What a view we'll have at sunset!'

'That was the idea,' she said. 'But come and see your bedroom.' She flung open the door with a flourish. 'Look! A walk-in cupboard, big enough to dress in. We'll put a mirror and chest on this side.'

'Whoever thought of knocking out a wall and making a place like this?' he demanded.

'I did. And why wouldn't I? For weeks the first thing I saw every morning was that awful row of hooks with clothes dangling on the wall. But you'll be really jealous when you see my room. We splurged a little. You'll need a decent guest room when the owners come. And being at the end they'll have privacy. It even has an outside door. See?'

'What a fine idea!' he said as he looked around the room. 'Did Neal and Max make those built-in chests and lockers? I wouldn't have believed it. Of course the idea was yours.'

'Mine and Alec's. We had a fresh inspiration almost every day. It's been such fun.'

'Has it really, Judy?' he asked.

'But I told you how I was looking forward to it. And I've barely started. Still have to paint and dress it up. Most of

78

the furniture is built. Neal's been working on it evenings in the tool shop.'

'And I'll be moving in soon?'

'If you don't mind the smell of paint—and the confusion. I'll try to hurry, Dad, and get you out of the bunkhouse as soon as I can.'

'But I don't want you to hurry. In fact I'd rather you wouldn't.' He laughed a little. 'Don't you see, Judy? It gives me such a good excuse to keep you here a bit longer.'

'An excuse! Are you that afraid of Aunt Nina? Why— why, she'll be delighted when she hears what I've been doing!'

'It's not Nina,' he said abruptly.

'Then,' she began, and stopped. Of course it was the Lady Luck. He hadn't mentioned it for so long she'd thought he'd thrust it from his mind, but she should have known he couldn't. 'You mean just because I changed my mind and—'

'Look, Judy, you had a well-planned summer when your discovery of what a mess I'd made of things brought you dashing up here in a panic.'

'But I didn't! And I wasn't in a panic! I'm having a marvellous time, and all you're thinking of is how soon you can send me back.'

'I'm regretting that I must,' he said. 'You know how wonderful it's been to have you here. I shouldn't have to tell you that.' He put his arm around her as they walked to the door. 'It's a grand house, Judy. When you write your Aunt Nina, tell her you've spoiled me completely for the hardships of a shack, and now I insist upon your staying until the place is finished.'

She watched him hurrying up the trail and wondered if he ever could forget the Lady Luck. She had thought all that was behind them. An overdeveloped conscience must be a dreadful thing. She wondered if she had one, then decided quite happily that she didn't. She wasn't even going to tell him that she intended to stay all summer.

Alec came in a half hour later. 'The Boss liked the house,' he said.

'He was crazy about it. But he's still brooding about the Lady Luck and how it brought me up here in the first place. Isn't he ever going to forget it, Alec?'

'Not in a few weeks! But it isn't eating him the way it was when you got here. Take it easy, Judy. He's a whole lot different. In the beginning all he thought about was work. When do you get your paint?'

'Rod said the order would be here in two weeks, and the *Resolute* called at Rampart Bay yesterday.'

'Funny the *Taku* didn't come in last night. Sang's nose was sure out of joint this morning. Had no eggs for breakfast.'

'Didn't you tell him Rod might bring them?'

'Rod's gone to Juneau. Spence told you that.'

'But he must be back by this time! Of course,' she added quickly, 'I don't know he is. He didn't tell me—' She stopped. Rod hadn't told her anything really, but he certainly wouldn't have said Admiralty Island if he was really going to Juneau. She didn't know why she was so sure of this. There was no reason he had to account to her for every little detail just because—and she thought of their afternoon above the crab flat. He needn't have told her about the fish pirates. It had taken courage and been wonderful of him and made something rather special of their friendship. And if he wanted Spence to think he'd gone to Juneau—he must have a perfectly good reason for it.

Alec walked over to the window. 'You were right about Rod's being back,' he said. 'I thought I heard his boat. I'll tell Sang his eggs have come.'

Sang had already started for the float, and when Judy and Alec reached it, the groceries were unloaded.

'I told Spence not to bother with them,' Rod explained. 'There wasn't any heavy freight, and I had to come down anyway.'

'Had to?' Judy repeated.

'Had to make sure those rubber boots fitted.'

'You mean they've come! And we can explore the river?'

'You've guessed it! I came early so we'd have a full day on the river.'

'Sang will pack a lunch,' she said.

Sang, about to depart under a load of groceries, turned to smile. 'I do him now,' he said. 'Fine lunch. Light away.'

Alec watched him scurrying up the earthen steps. 'That's the first time I ever heard him say "right away" instead of "by-and-by". Was it just the eggs or did you bring him something special?'

'Strawberries.' Rod laughed. 'But don't let Jim, the sawmill cook, hear about it or Charlie Reynolds and I will be in trouble. Didn't you like Charlie?'

'We sure did,' Alec said. 'Wish I'd known about his sawmill when I came, so I could have given him the business instead of having all the stuff towed down from Juneau.'

'Charlie's one of the finest fellows on this coast,' Rod said. 'But he's so afraid someone might guess it, he's always grouching about something or other.'

'He didn't while he was here,' Alec said with some vehemence. 'And a lot of his ideas make real sense. If everybody thought—'

'Dad said he had an unusually original mind,' Judy broke in quickly. Alec was apt to be a bit belligerent in his defence of anyone he admired.

'Charlie takes his own slant at everything,' Rod said. 'One of the things I like best about him.'

'Did the paint come?' Judy asked.

'Yesterday. Just got under the wire. The house was the first thing I saw when I came through the entrance. It looks great! Here's your mail sack.'

Alec opened it. 'Five letters for you, Judy. One for me. A few for the crew, and all the rest are for the Boss.'

She shuffled through the envelopes. The thick one was from Aunt Nina, the others from classmates. They had all promised faithfully to write to each other, and now, more than a month since she'd left Boston, she hadn't written to one of them.

They carried the packages to the cabin, where Judy left Alec to show Rod the magnificence of the built-in features while she changed for the day up-river. But first she read Aunt Nina's letter, which she'd dreaded a bit despite her reassurances to her father. Aunt Nina might be disapproving, or even worse, feel hurt.

The letter, however, was neither. Not only did she understand Judy's abrupt departure but even applauded her giving up a Bar Harbour summer for a visit with her father. 'I know how overjoyed David must be,' she wrote. 'He's seen so little of you, but of course he knew that, living in mining camps, nothing else was possible. Now, with these weeks together, you have a chance to catch up with one another.' She was concerned about the loneliness of Shaman Cove. 'With no young people of your age and David always so absorbed in his work, you'll have many empty days.' She had already thought of books, had mailed a package, and would send on any others Judy wanted.

She had received a very charming letter from Mrs. Fellows to whom she had written explaining the sudden change in plans. 'Rushing off as you did, I wasn't sure whether you'd already done so,' she wrote. 'But Mrs Fellows understood it perfectly and thinks it was quite wonderful of you to realize how lonely an Alaskan mining camp would be for your father. She's very fond of you, Judy, and hopes you can join them later, but I told her I was expecting you to come to me. As usual, I'll close the house on Labour Day, but you'll surely be back long before then. I'm so glad you and David are having this time together to talk about your winter plans. It is so much more satisfactory than trying to do it in letters.'

She went on with news of Judy's friends, the girls who were going to college and those who were to make their debuts. 'I imagine David would be gratified if you decided on college, although to me you've never seemed exactly the type who would. And Boston will be very gay this winter with so many coming-out parties for girls you know. Natalie Benson will be married in October. She seems so young, although she is eighteen. Of course she and Robert have been devoted since perambulator days, and both families are very happy about the marriage. Natalie wants you as one of her bridesmaids, and naturally I assured her you'd be delighted.'

Judy finished the letter, replaced it in the envelope, and put it on her father's desk. If anything could reassure him about her visit, Aunt Nina's letter ought to do it. The letter was so like her—poised, urbane and, as always, loving. Aunt Nina might live an ordered life, but the sudden dash to Alaska hadn't disturbed her in the slightest, and Judy thought she should have known it wouldn't. People like Aunt Nina, with stability and balance, were never thrown off stride by the unexpected. They had perspective, always knew that eventually their world would return to law and order. And usually it did.

Judy changed to dungarees. The hip boots fitted perfectly. She turned the tops down into jaunty cuffs, which gave her something of the look of a cavalier. But she liked the general effect.

Apparently the others did too.

Alec laughed. 'She's wearing 'em fisherman-style already.'

'I thought it was Alaskan,' Judy said. 'It's the way Rod wears his. Besides it's much more comfortable.' Rod's stare of frank approval was making her a bit self-conscious. 'Isn't that why you do it, Rod?'

'It's a good enough reason,' he said. 'And don't let Alec bother you. You look great in that outfit, Judy. Ready to start?'

They crossed the bay, left the skiff at the beach, and climbed the steep cliff beside the falls. It was green and very refreshing so near the cascade of water, and the cliff was terraced by small rock gardens. Half-way up, Judy sat down beside a particularly lovely one. Waist-high ferns made a frieze as a background while huge bluebells nodded at the edge. A mist from the waterfall floated past them, and iridescent droplets hurled themselves free from the flashing column to leap to the pool below. Judy thought she'd come here often.

'If it weren't for my new boots and knowing there's a river above, I wouldn't go on,' she said. 'It's so peaceful up here, looking down at everything.'

Rod put out a hand and lifted her to her feet. 'Come on before you get too lazy.'

They climbed until they were above the falls and found the river surprisingly quiet. They had only to wade around the outside of a large deep pool to reach the shallow channel where they splashed happily up midstream between green banks of alder and trailing berry bushes.

Never before had Judy walked up a river, and at first she was too enchanted with the sparkling water rushing over white gravel, the tug of the current at her legs, and the need too of maintaining balance, to look around her. Then suddenly she became aware of the broad river valley stretching off to the forested slopes of mountains. And rising above the green slopes were turreted battlements of rough-hewn granite, topped by glistening snow peaks with cloud shadows playing on them.

She drew in her breath. 'No wonder you said I didn't know Alaska until I'd seen the rivers! This—this—' and she waved her arm to include the mountains and the valley—'this is wonderful.'

Rod smiled. 'I was afraid you didn't like it. You hadn't said a word.'

'Are all the rivers as beautiful?'

'Not all, but they're all different. That's the fun of going up them. You never know what you're going to find around a bend.' And then he suddenly called, 'Look out! It'll be deep at that big boulder where the current cuts in. Give me your hand.'

He negotiated it easily with a few inches of rubber boot to spare, but even though Judy tried to walk on tiptoe, water sloshed in over hers.

'Ouch!' she screamed as the icy water filled her boots. 'It's cold!'

'Melted snow, fresh off the peaks,' he said. 'We'll hunt a spot where you can dry your feet.'

Presently when the river made a sharp bend around a flat ledge, they found exactly what they were looking for. It was a perfect place to bail out rubber boots and eat lunch. They sat on a rock and talked. Rod told her of young Jeff's arrival and the excitement of the grandparents and his mother's wanting him to bring her to Hidden Harbour.

'Wish I could take you,' he said. 'But it's a good six hours trip from Shaman Cove.'

'And I'd like to know your mother. Charlie Reynolds said such wonderful things about her. Doesn't she come to Rampart on steamer day? I'll be there often in the motor boat.'

'Mean you've learned to run it!' he exclaimed.

'It's easy. Not half as tricky as an automobile. Only Dad is still suffering from clutch fright. But after I've proved I can make a proper landing at your float, Alec has promised to make me skipper of the *Working Stiff.*'

'Hurrah! And I'd been worrying about how I was ever going to see you! It's been a long time, Judy.'

'Ages,' she agreed. 'But you told me you would be away.'

'And since then with trollers in every evening and'—he paused—'a second trip to Admiralty— Well, between trying to run a store and—and everything—'

'You must have been busy,' she finished for him. She was relieved he'd said Admiralty instead of Juneau, but evidently he didn't want to talk about it. 'Aren't you hungry?' she asked. 'I am. I hope Sang has packed enough.'

The lunch was more than enough. Sang had outdone himself in honour of the strawberries. Rod chuckled when he saw crab salad.

'I take it you've been hunting.'

'It's my favourite sport,' she said. 'I introduced Dad and Alec to it. They liked it, but I know they didn't have the fun you and I did.'

He laughed, and then their eyes met in a wordless acknowledgement of what that afternoon had meant. It had been the real beginning of their friendship.

'Spence told me he spent an evening at your camp and had a grand time,' Rod said.

'Yes, and everybody liked him.' She knew Rod would want to hear this. 'Alec loved the story about how he got the *Taku.*'

'Alec would understand what it took to spend your last cent buying a boat off the bottom when no one thought you had a chance to raise it,' Rod said. 'Spence is quite a fellow, Judy.'

'I know,' she said.

Dependable and steady was what Daniels had said about Spence, and undoubtedly he was. But this needn't mean that Rod wasn't. Dependable, certainly, she thought, but steady wasn't exactly the word to use for Rod. Intense perhaps, and strung tight, almost as though ideas were boiling up inside of him that made plain steady seem a little humdrum. She'd never known anyone who was such a strange contradiction. But his aliveness made him an exciting person to be with.

They finished lunch, and Judy leaned back against a windfall in a languor of deep content. Beside them the river sang a lilting melody as it ran over gravelled riffles, and in an eddy below a mother duck was giving her young brood their first lesson in fishing for a living. She had apparently concluded Rod and Judy were to be permanent fixtures of the scene, and Judy felt a bit that way. Her zeal for exploration had evaporated completely.

'Whatever the river does above here, it can't be any nicer than this,' she remarked a little tentatively.

'And we have to leave some stretches for next time,' Rod said with some alacrity, then settled down beside her against the windfall.

She smiled and thought how comfortable it was to be able to say 'next time' to each other without making too much of it. At school, dates had been of great importance. At least, any girl had to have enough of them to maintain her self-respect, but dates were different somehow from merely knowing you were going to do things together because you both enjoyed it.

'Did you know the pink run is on?' he asked. 'Started with a bang, and the cannery is running full blast '

'And you promised to show me a salmon river.'

'I was wondering which one I'd take you to,' he said.

'Are there so many?'

'Many! With millions of fish on their way to home streams! I'm sure I told you what pink salmon means to Alaska!'

'You did. And so did Charlie Reynolds. He was explaining to Alec, of all people, that pink salmon, and not gold, were the real riches of this country. For a moment I was afraid it was going to be the end of a beautiful friendship.'

He laughed and said he would have liked to have heard it. 'But Charlie's right. Why, salmon was what this country lived on even before there were any canneries. Look how easy our Indians had it. All the food they wanted just for the taking. You know, Phil Trent says it was salmon that probably accounted for our famous Tlingit art. With no trouble in getting food, they had time to make all sorts of decorations for their houses and their ceremonial feasts and dances. They could spend the whole winter weaving and carving.'

'Really!' she exclaimed. One never knew what odd fact Rod would turn up next, but with a sister married to a New York artist, he would know such things.

'And Alaska still lives on salmon,' he went on. 'We don't have to eat it, but the canneries and boats and traps all pay taxes. Charlie Reynolds is always grouching about salmon money leaving this country, but the lumber for wharves and boats and canneries keeps his sawmill going. Without salteries and canneries Spence could never have built up a freight line. Nor would the Tlingits be able to buy motor boats and sewing machines and phonographs— things they'd never dreamed of owning. Why, even our brown bears that bring big-game hunters up here every year depend on the pink run. Wait for it just as much as any canner.'

'Now, you're making that up!'

'But I'm not!' he insisted. 'They know when it's time to move down from the high country and begin to take life easy on a salmon stream. They can catch a fish any time they're hungry and put on fat for the winter. Don't ask me how they know, but they arrive about the same time as the pinks. Once in a while you may see an odd bear on the river before the run begins, but Jeff says he only takes a look, then starts right back up the mountain. Maybe he's a scout for the others, but more likely he's just one of those wise

87

old fellows who believes in finding things out for himself.'

'Does the run start the same time on all the rivers?'

'It's different in different districts, but it's usually the same time every year on each river. I don't know why. I wish I did. There are a lot of things I wish I knew. I'd like to know where the pinks spend those two years while they're out to sea and if the fish from each river stick together.'

'But someone must know!'

'Seems so, doesn't it,' Rod said quietly. 'But Alan Knox —he was the fish scientist aboard the *Cytherea*—said they didn't. I spent a lot of time with him when they were in Rampart, and ever since then he's sent me books and bulletins. He's a professor at Stanford University.'

Judy stared, visibly impressed. Rod was talking like a science graduate. 'You mean you've really tried to study fish?'

'Not fish! Pink salmon!'

'I see,' she said.

She didn't see, but evidently Rod wasn't anxious to explain. She watched him plucking lichen from a rock and carefully piling it in a little heap. The project seemed to have his entire attention. Then he looked up suddenly.

'What kind of a river do you want to see?' he asked. 'A big run with fish crowding the whole stream or—a river with a—a sort of history?'

She considered, trying to guess if her choice held any importance. 'A big run would be exciting,' she began, 'but a river with a history—that sounds— What sort of history?'

'It used to be one of the finest salmon streams on the coast. Long ago. The old carver—you know, the one I told you about who took care of me when—' He hesitated, and she nodded quickly. 'He and his wife, Jennie, talked a lot about the old days when the Indians from the whole district always went there to smoke their winter salmon. Afterwards I got to thinking about it. People around here said Tallac River had been fished out, but that didn't make good sense. The Tlingits couldn't have fished out a stream like that in a hundred years! There had to be some other reason. So Shagoon-e-ish and I went down there!'

'And that's what you were doing on Admiralty Island?' she said.

'Not this time. More than two years ago—when I first started thinking about the river.'

She looked at him, puzzled. 'But why? When you didn't know the river and all this happened so long ago?'

'Why did I care?' he asked. 'I don't know.' He stared off over the river for a moment. 'I guess—' he went on, 'I was beginning to throw out my chest again, and with even the old canners taking it for granted Tallac River had been fished out, I wanted to know. Just their saying so didn't make it true!' He told what he had found and about the clearing of the river. 'This must sound sort of crazy to you.' He glanced at her briefly. 'Me, a kid, thinking I knew more than the old canners. Why, Daniels would have laughed if I'd tried to tell him. And it would be two years before I could prove that I was right.'

'And were you?' she demanded. 'Of course you were!'

'How'd you guess?'

'When you came this morning, I think I knew something grand had happened to you. You were different, somehow. And how wonderful for you! It's—it's like the end of the story—the story you told me that afternoon.' She knew it wouldn't hurt him to be reminded of it now. 'But the right ending and the true one!' There were tears in her eyes as she smiled up at him, so proud and so happy for him.

'That's how I hoped you'd feel about it.' His voice was husky. 'It all fits together somehow.'

And then his arms were around her, and their lips met in a pledge of faith and confidence. As they drew apart, Judy thought the kiss had been so right, so natural. Anything less would have belittled the glowing sense of his achievement. For a moment they sat staring at the river. It was Rod who finally broke the silence.

'I wanted to tell you where I was going that last afternoon. But I couldn't. Not even Spence or Jeff knew about Tallac. Besides, right then, there wasn't much of anything to tell.'

'There was a lot to tell—even if—even if you hadn't been

right about the reason!' she said vehemently. 'Wouldn't you have told me that?'

'I don't know.' He thought about it for a moment. 'Perhaps,' he said. 'But I'd have hated having you feel sorry for me. Anyway you know it now, and you and Spence and Jeff, and Mom, of course, are the only ones who do. I hadn't intended to tell you today. Wanted to make it a real surprise and wait until we had our licences for trap sites.'

'Trap sites? You don't mean for salmon traps?'

'Sure. One in Jeff's name, the other in Spence's. Lucky for us, he's of age and can get a licence.'

'But Rod!' she gasped. 'You said salmon traps cost thousands of dollars! And Mr Daniels told us—'

'They won't cost us what they'd cost a cannery. And Daniels will jump at the chance to loan the money on sites like those! He'll only wish he had them!'

The idea of Mr Daniels joyfully loaning Rod thousands of dollars was startling. Then as Rod explained this was the ordinary procedure, it began to seem more reasonable. And in a salmon trap, unlike a store, Rod and Mr Daniels shared a common objective. Also Spence, whom the canner admired, would be a partner in the venture.

'Daniels knows we can pay it back the first season,' Rod said. 'Those traps earn real money. Why, some of them have caught a million fish a season. Of course, next year won't be a big run. But the year after, when this summer's spawn comes back to homestream!' His eyes glowed with little pinpoints of excitement. 'I don't dare think about it, Judy!'

'You mean it would be like the old days on Tallac River?'

'Maybe not. I don't know how long it might take to build up a river. I wish I did. But if we didn't get a million fish, or anywhere near that, think what even a good catch would mean. Mom and Jeff—they've had tough going. They knew it would be tough when they loaded us aboard the old sloop and sailed off for Alaska. But that didn't stop them! And now—well—they ought to have their chance to take it easy.'

She smiled at him. The vision of a million fish had been beyond her imagination, but traps translated into comfort and security took on real meaning. 'Was that the reason you had to try it—even though you knew you might not be right?'

'Partly,' he said. 'They're my family, aren't they?' And then he added, 'But it wasn't the only reason. You know, Judy, there's a lot to be proved about Alaska salmon. The canners aren't proving anything. They're only thinking about this season's pack. They get a bad year, and they blame the trout, the sea lions, the eagles, even the Indians —everything but themselves for not letting enough fish through to seed the rivers for a crop two years later. The way they're going at it—some day we won't have any salmon.'

He leapt to his feet and paced up and down in his excitement.

'But if we did it right—why—we could have pink runs forever! Only the canners can't see it. They figure any fish they don't catch some other fellow will, so they go on fighting each other for a bigger pack instead of thinking about the salmon. What we need are laws to stop this overfishing and then make sure the laws are kept. Why, we've only had an Alaskan Bureau of Fisheries in Juneau for eight years, and they still haven't enough boats or men to make inspections.

'I don't say I know now what the laws should be. But if a little thing like clearing out a channel can bring back a salmon stream, think what it might mean if we were to shut off a whole district where the runs are dwindling and give the pinks a chance to build up again. There're a lot of things we could do. But we have to do them before it's too late. We're a rich country, Judy, but we won't be if we don't take care of what we have.'

'You mean like the Forest Service does.'

'Sure. I've been thinking about it lately. There'd be a lot of satisfaction in a job like that.' He put out a hand to help her up. 'It's time I was starting for Rampart if I aim to get in before the trollers. But you're coming up on boat day?' She nodded. 'Good! Spence will be back from Juneau with the licences. We'll have plenty to celebrate. Two trap sites. And your first run as skipper.'

8

WHEN THE *Working Stiff* had cleared the entrance to Rampart Bay, Judy blew a long blast on the whistle, and almost at once she saw Rod running to the float to meet them.

'Need help on the landing?' her father asked. Until then his passenger manners had been perfect.

'Not a bit,' she said. 'I was only making sure of my public.'

'Fair enough,' he said, 'especially after the performance I staged last time.'

But she knew he had guessed her speech had been pure boasting. Inwardly she was in a panic as she made a turn to come in for a port landing. When close to the float, she went into reverse, then threw the wheel hard over and jerked out the clutch. The *Working Stiff* laid neatly alongside.

Rod let out a yell of triumph. 'Came in like a whisper! You could teach these trollers something! Where'd you learn that trick?'

'From Alec. And you're no more surprised than I am that it worked.' She was finding success a bit intoxicating, and she looked inquiringly at her father.

'I'm sufficiently impressed.' David Randolph stepped on to the float and shook hands with Rod. 'That landing alone should win her skipper's papers. Is Spence around?'

'In the store talking to Mom and Jeff. Spence was on his way to the boat works, but you can catch him if you hurry.'

David Randolph nodded and started off. Rod made the *Working Stiff* fast and came aboard.

'You got the licences!' she said. 'I knew it the minute I saw you.'

'Two sites! Spence got in this morning, and nobody knows he's even been to Juneau. The fellows at the fishery bureau didn't bother to ask why he wanted them. A couple of floating traps more or less was all it meant to them. So we're safe on that.'

'Safe?'

'From the news of the run leaking out from Juneau. If Daniels ever heard a whisper, he'd have that bay so full of purse seiners the rest of the Tallac pinks would never get upriver. Fish it this year, and we'd be back where we started!'

'But if he loans the money, won't you have to tell him about Tallac?'

'When the run is over. It isn't a big one, and it's bound to dwindle off.'

'And you won't know until the run is over if you can build those traps! How can you stand it? Waiting for weeks —and weeks—'

'But we know we're going to build them.' Then he glanced at her sharply. 'What makes you think Daniels won't loan the money?'

'I never said that!' she protested. 'And what would I know about it? I've only seen him once.' She realized she sounded unnecessarily vehement. 'It's only—your having to wait so long without being actually certain—the way you could be if you could only talk to him about it. I'd hate that. I suppose I'm like my father,' she went on after a moment. 'Having to be sure of everything. He's—he's fanatical about it. And so—' She let the sentence trail off unfinished. It had been pointless anyway. Rod didn't know about the Lady Luck, and it would be difficult to explain it to him.

'I'm so glad your mother came today,' she said. 'And Jeff.'

'They got here in time for breakfast. Jeff couldn't wait to hear the news. Never saw him so steamed up before. He's having a hard time not to show it.'

'And no wonder! With news like that! I'm just waiting until it's all right to tell Father. He'd understand about the river and how you just had to find out why the pinks stopped coming. In a way it's sort of like his work—discovering what made things happen.'

'Only he knows exactly how to go about it,' Rod said. 'A lot of times I've wished I did.'

In the store they found David Randolph still talking to the Bairds. Spence waved as Judy entered.

'Hi, Judy!' he called. 'Hear you've got your skipper's papers. And you earned them with that landing!'

'Did you see it?' Judy asked. Spence was nice to have spoken of it. No one managed a motor boat the way he did. And he must have stayed just to congratulate her, for he departed for the boat works a moment later. Mary Baird smiled and made room on the bench beside her.

'Jeff's been telling me a wonderful story about their voyage to Alaska,' her father said. 'I'm sorry you missed it, Judy. They came up here long before there were any motor boats.'

'The trip took us weeks and weeks,' Mary said. 'But Jeff loved every minute of it.'

'Didn't notice you and the young 'uns had such a bad time.' Jeff chuckled. 'It was Alaska or bust with all of us. Do you sail, Judy?'

'No,' she said. 'Of course I've gone sailing, but I'm not a sailor, really. Dad was though, when he was younger. And he doesn't like motor boats either.'

'I knew right off your father was a man of sense,' Jeff said. 'When I need a motor boat to get me to Hidden Harbour, I'll stay home by my own fire.'

'And let Spence and me run your errands?' Rod asked with a grin.

'You caught me there, lad,' Jeff admitted. 'Guess I wouldn't like that either.'

It was all the carefree banter of heightened spirits, but Judy sensed that underneath Rod's family were exactly as she had imagined they would be. She liked Jeff even better than she had expected to. He wasn't trying to be a quaint wilderness character and different from other people. He was only being himself, and Mary Baird was precisely what Charlie Reynolds had said she was—warm and steady and understanding, a person one was drawn to instantly. Judy had an odd conviction that Aunt Nina and Mary Baird would understand and like each other.

Presently David Randolph stood up. 'Wish I didn't have to break up this visit, but I must send off a cable. How about transportation to the cannery, Judy?'

'Not in a motor boat when a sloop is doing nothing!' Jeff exclaimed in horror. 'We'll go over there in style.'

Mary Baird watched them depart. 'Jeff's so pleased to have discovered another sailor.'

'Don't you sail?' Judy asked.

For a moment Mary Baird seemed somewhat startled. 'I've never had to! There's always been someone else to do it—Jeff or Spence or Vicky and—'

'She's not an outdoor woman, are you, Mom?' Rod grinned and put his arm around her. He appeared to think he'd paid her a tribute.

'But you mustn't tell anyone! The idea of making your mother out a fraud!' There was an infectious gaiety in her laughter. 'And you were right, Rod, about Judy reminding one of Vicky, even though they haven't the same colouring, and Judy is much prettier. I think it's the way they hold their heads.' She turned to Judy. 'Rod spoke of it when he told us about your being here this summer, and I've been hoping he would bring you to Hidden Harbour.'

'If Judy doesn't mind coming up to Rampart by herself, we could get an early start and be there in time for dinner,' Rod said. 'Do you suppose, Mom, you could pack a lunch so we could go upriver? Judy's never seen a brown bear, and I'd like to show her one. Is the same old gang fishing there this summer?'

'Jeff was up the other day. That big she-bear who thinks she owns the second riffles has two cubs again this summer. She's just as fine a fisherman as ever. Jeff watched her a long time. I think she made him feel a little lonesome, remembering that her picture was the first one Vicky ever sold.'

'You mean she actually took pictures of brown bears!' Judy exclaimed. 'I've always heard they were dangerous.'

'Not with Jeff and his gun along,' Mary Baird said. 'He always went with Vicky. He'd much rather watch a brown bear having its picture taken than shoot one. Do you use a camera, Judy?'

'I'm not a real photographer like Vicky, but of course I brought a camera with me to Alaska.'

'Then you should certainly have a brown bear picture.'

'You mean I could take one?' Judy asked. The idea of photographing the biggest bear in the world had never occurred to her.

'Not in just an hour or two. We might not even see a bear in that time. But is there any reason to hurry back to Shaman Cove? Can't you stay over?'

'Why—why—' Judy began, overcome with surprise and pleasure. 'I'd love to, Mrs Baird! Only— I don't want to be a nuisance.'

'We'd love to have you. Hidden Harbour is much too far to come for just a few hours. You and Jeff need a whole day upriver to get good pictures.'

'Why didn't I think of that in the first place!' Rod said. 'Then I can run down to Shaman Cove and get you, Judy, so the mine won't be without a boat. Be all right, Mom, if we waited for a couple of weeks, when I'm not so busy, before we come?'

Judy knew he was thinking of trips he'd have to make to Tallac River and didn't dare look at his mother for fear her own eyes would betray knowledge of their secret. 'And I must paint our cabin,' she said. 'Poor Dad! He's been sleeping in the bunkhouse because *I* had to use his room.'

'Come whenever you can,' Mary Baird said. 'Jeff and I are always home, and the brown bears will be there until September. Here's the *Resolute* coming through the entrance.'

They were all on the float when the steamship turned in for a landing. Judy watched the ship make fast, the cargo doors open, and freight begin to pour from the hold. It seemed that everyone in Rampart Bay was there, hoping for a first chance at the vegetables and meat. Rod checked shipments, signed manifests, and directed merchandise to the freight shed or the store. Customers trundled crates and boxes. Captain Scott called greetings from the bridge to old friends and exchanged bits of coastal gossip. It was an exciting touch with the world outside.

'I wouldn't have missed this for anything!' Judy exclaimed. 'Of course,' she added, 'it's my first boat day.'

'It's still exciting to me,' Mary Baird said. 'When we

first came, there was no boat at Rampart. It's only since we've had a cannery this has been a steamship stop. So—' and her glance included the *Resolute* and the busy scene around her—'this seems very wonderful. Mail and supplies, coming in each week!'

'But whatever did you do before?'

'We had to sail to the Indian villages, either Hoonah or Killisnoo. Sometimes in winter we couldn't go for months and months. You see our first sloop, the one we sailed to Alaska wasn't very able. It was an old boat when Jeff bought it, but it was all we could afford.' She turned to speak to Jim, the sawmill cook, and introduce him. 'And I'm sure Miss Randolph hopes to have some of those melons you are hauling. Would eight be enough, Judy?'

'I'll pick out some good ones,' Jim said. 'And how about you, Mrs Baird? I came over to ask if you didn't want a couple.'

'If you can spare them. Will that leave plenty for the sawmill?' She turned to Judy. 'Jim is so wonderful about helping Rod with vegetables. Are the tomatoes good this week, Jim?'

'Best yet. Do you want some? And you too, Miss?' They nodded. 'I'll put aside a few baskets before they're all gone. How big's the mine crew?'

'Fourteen. And Father and me, of course.'

He dashed off on his errand. Judy breathed a sigh of relief. As official shopper for the mine crew she'd been having stage fright, and now her strongest competitor for choice items was not only disarmed but anxious to be helpful. 'Isn't he wonderful,' she said, then smiled. 'Or rather you are, Mrs Baird. No wonder Charlie Reynolds raves about you.'

'Poor Charlie!' Mary Baird laughed. 'He doesn't dare say *boo* in his own cook camp. But Jim enjoys doing favours for people if they'll only let him. He's managed the vegetables on boat days for so long he's come to believe they all belong to him.'

The *Working Stiff* was stowed and waiting long before the sloop arrived with Jeff and David Randolph.

'Had a fine sail around the harbour,' Jeff announced.

'So we noticed,' his wife said. 'We were thinking we'd have to send out a rescue party for Mr Randolph.'

'But I enjoyed it!' he protested. 'The sloop foots beautifully! I wouldn't have imagined she could sail so close to the wind. And she handles like a dream.'

'Jeff, don't forget to tell that to Tom Walsh!' Mary said. 'It would make him so happy. Tom's the man who built it for us,' she explained to David Randolph.

'It's a fine job. Perhaps when you come next summer, Judy, you and I will have a sloop. I might make a sailor of you yet.'

The Bairds saw them off, and Judy hoped the departure of the *Working Stiff* was as spirited as its arrival. As they went through the entrance, Rod was still on the float and waving. They were well down the strait before her father finished his deckhand duties and joined her at the wheel.

'That Jeff Baird is a great old boy,' he said. 'I'm glad I had a chance for a real talk with him. I'd had a different picture of him—just an impression, of course. Probably from something Daniels might have said about the family.'

'I don't think Mr Daniels knows them very well.'

'And he wouldn't understand a man like Jeff, anyway. I liked Mrs Baird too. Quite an unusual woman, I thought, but you saw more of her than I did.'

'And she's wonderful! I was sure she would be from things Rod had told me. She's invited me to Hidden Harbour for a visit.'

'She has! It would be a nice change for you. Going, aren't you?'

She nodded. 'A little later when Rod has—' She stopped. 'I mean I told her I wanted to finish the cabin first. And there's no hurry. The brown bears will be on the river all summer. I'm going to take my camera and get pictures of them fishing. Imagine me getting a photograph of the biggest game in America trying to catch his dinner.'

'Brown bears!' he exclaimed. 'But they're dangerous, Judy.'

'Jeff is going to take me. He always went with Vicky.'

'Oh, that's quite different,' her father said, looking much relieved. 'I'm sure he's a man you can depend on. He's really a remarkable individual, Judy. Surprising too. At least he was to me. I'd been presuming all this talk about the Bairds was because of their isolation and that he was just an ordinary woodsman.'

'Why?'

'Possibly I'd been judging by other odd characters I've run across in out-of-the-way places. Drifters usually, and generally they've been failures on the outside. On the whole I'd found them rather opinionated and generally boring. So you see'—and he smiled at her—'it wasn't that I'm easily impressed.'

'I knew you liked Jeff when you two came back from sailing! And usually you don't—I mean usually you—'

'Don't what?' he asked. 'Don't like people?'

'Of course you do. Look at you and Alec! All I meant was that usually it takes you longer to make up your mind about strangers—especially if they're a bit odd and sort of—well, romantic, like Jeff.'

He laughed. 'I am a bit wary of the too colourful,' he admitted. 'But it was more than liking for Jeff. There's something rather magnificent about him and his search for a new frontier that held a challenge. Hidden Harbour wasn't an escape. It was a goal. Jeff is a natural firster.'

'There must have been a lot of them in America that nobody ever heard of.'

'Those ahead of the pioneers, like the mountain men. I've always thought there was something poetic in their story, and I find it in old Jeff when he tells how compelling his urge was. It's hard to explain, Judy, but I had a distinct feeling that he is a man of bigger vision than we often meet. Stubborn, yes. But right or wrong, nothing has swerved him from his path.'

9

JUDY LOOKED around their living-room, at her father reading in the chair she had upholstered with excelsior, at the softly shaded lamps, at the big table with magazines and books, and felt a glow of satisfaction. The room was even more attractive than she had dared to hope it would be. Even the couch looked actually luxurious with its array of bright pillows. She'd made them and the curtains in the week of steady rain.

Alaska, she'd discovered, was not always gold and blue and sparkling, which was fortunate if one had a job to finish. When it was drenched in sunlight, the land was too inviting and there were so many things to do. Trips to Rampart Bay, explorations of the river, food to gather. She and Rod had kept the camp supplied with crabs and clams. He had come often, usually with the excuse of a big king salmon or a fresh halibut from a fishing schooner, and once he had appeared at breakfast to announce it was a fine day for a picnic.

'I have to go to an Indian camp on Admiralty Island, and Judy's never seen a salmon stream,' he'd explained to her father.

Judy, knowing Rod must mean Tallac River, tried to appear as casual as he was about the expedition, and luckily her father asked no questions, only said Daniels had told him the canneries were expecting a big season.

At Tallac Bay, Rod showed her the blazed trees above the Baird sites, and somehow the blazes made the traps seem much more real. When they went upriver, Sha-goon-e-ish reported that the run was already beginning to fall off, but to Judy it was enthralling. They sat beside a gravelled riffle and watched the fish rest in the pool below to gather strength for the battle against the current and then depart in a concerted rush. Their thrashing tails and writhing bodies beat the shallow water and sent spray flying in their instinctive urge to reach spawning ground.

These were the salmon that would seed the river for a harvest two years later, and, except for Rod, this could never have been. Afterwards, she wished so often she was free to tell her father of that day. He had caught the poetic quality in Jeff's compelling search for an unspoiled country, and surely he would see something of that same spirit in what Rod had done to save a river. She was thinking about it this evening as they sat in their new living-room.

Her father put down his book and smiled at her. 'You've been admiring your handiwork for the last half hour, and I don't wonder you're smirky. It's a grand job, Judy. I'll have a real home this winter. But I'm going to miss you.'

He hadn't mentioned her departure since the morning they'd inspected the house together, and for a moment she was startled. The days had slipped so easily into weeks it didn't seem possible it was already mid-August.

'There's no reason for rushing off,' she said. 'Aunt Nina knows I'm staying on, and I've already told her I don't want a coming-out party.'

'I hope she wasn't disappointed. It was a generous thing to have offered.'

'Wasn't it!' she said. 'But she agrees it would be rather silly to be a debutante in Boston when I have a father living in Alaska. It isn't as though I didn't have a family—and a very nice one too.' She smiled at him. 'Besides, it's always bothered her that we saw so little of each other.'

'It's bothered me,' he said, 'but I couldn't help it, Judy. You've understood this, haven't you?' She nodded. 'I've always hoped you did. And this summer— I've realized more than ever how much I've missed.'

'And so have I, Dad.' She smiled happily. 'That's one of the nicest things you've ever said to me.'

'Seems I'm not a very articulate fellow. But your rushing up here the way you did just because you thought I was in trouble!' His eyes were tender. 'I've thought about it a lot, Judy. It's the one good thing that came out of the Lady Luck. For a long time I've meant to tell you.'

'Really! Then—' She hesitated, hardly daring to ask the

question, and yet she had to know. 'Then—the Lady Luck doesn't bother you any more?'

'It bothers me, of course, Judy. That's only natural. But you took the worst hurt out when you managed to make me believe that I hadn't spoiled your summer. That was the most important thing.'

'I know,' she said. 'If it hadn't been for the Lady Luck, you wouldn't have been so stirred up about it.' It was a good deal like saying if he hadn't had a cold, he wouldn't have sneezed, but she was sure she could say this now.

'Perhaps I wouldn't have,' he admitted. 'What have you and Nina decided about this winter?'

'Nothing definite,' she said slowly. 'Does it make any difference to you just when I go east for my visit?'

'Only that later I'll have to be in California on business, and you can't stay here alone.'

'I could go with you. You know, Dad, I've been thinking —if you're going to be in Alaska, I'd rather stay in the west. While we're in California, I could find out about a college, like—like Stanford.'

'It's a good school, but what made you think of Stanford? Any special reason?'

'No. Except I've been hearing a lot about it. Spence told me Chris Daniels goes there.' She didn't add that Rod had said some day he hoped to take a special course on fish, but she reflected quickly this wasn't her reason really.

'But, Judy, in an eastern school you'd be near your Aunt Nina and people you've always known. That means a great deal to a girl. And as yet I'm not even sure I'll stay in Alaska. There's nothing definite about this as a mine.'

'Of course! We don't have to settle anything yet. I only told you so you'd know I had been really thinking about my future. I was afraid you thought I hadn't.'

Judy had tried to form a picture of what Hidden Harbour would be like, but the reality was completely different. Rod's boat swung around the point, and the harbour lay before her, a small green cup held among the mountains. She caught her breath in sheer delight. Here was beauty she had not imagined. A little world set apart, serene, secluded, but its isolation brought no sense of loneliness.

A sloop rode at its mooring. The flat at the river mouth was riotous with Indian paintbrush and goldenrod against the deep blue of tall lupin. The house stood on a broad bench above the water, overlooking the bay, the river, and the welter of peaks beyond. It was not a log cabin, as Judy had expected, at least nothing like those she'd seen pictured. Its long, low lines gave it an air of graciousness; it seemed to have grown there, as did the stand of spruce behind it.

Mary Baird had heard the boat and ran down the path to meet them. 'I never dreamed you could be here so early,' she said as she kissed them. 'But I'm so glad you are.'

'I was at Shaman Cove before the crew had finished breakfast,' Rod said.

When they went inside, Judy thought how exactly right was the big main room, which served as kitchen and living quarters. It belonged in such a house. As she helped Mary set the table, she looked around in unconcealed delight.

'This is the first log house I've ever been in,' she explained. 'I never dreamed they could be so lovely. Just look at the colour of those big timbers!'

'That's age, not paint,' Rod said. 'Eleven years, isn't it, Mom? And another year before that while they were drying enough so Jeff was willing to start building.'

'He wanted this to last a lifetime,' his mother said. 'And I know it will. Long after Jeff or I will have any need for it. Can't you stay over, Rod, and go upriver with them tomorrow?'

Rod shook his head. 'Wish I could. And I have to start back early enough to stop off and see Jeff. Where's he working?'

'In Indian Cove. Half-way up the mountain.'

'I'll run in there and blow the whistle. He won't mind coming down when he hears the news. The Tallac run is over, and we don't have to keep it quiet any longer. It was already beginning to fall off the day I took Judy up to see it.'

Judy stared at Rod in amazement. Now his mother

couldn't help but know he had revealed their secret to an outsider, but she appeared to think this only natural as she turned to Judy.

'Then you didn't see a real run? That's too bad. Is the river pretty? I've never been there.'

'I thought it was lovely. And even if it wasn't a big run, it was terribly exciting.'

'I could hardly get her to stop watching long enough to eat the lunch Jennie cooked for us!' Rod laughed. 'And you know, Mom, the first thing Jennie said was how much Judy looked like Vicky.'

'From Jennie that was a real compliment, my dear,' his mother said. 'Vicky's been her favourite ever since the children first went to the village.'

Rod departed soon after dinner. Judy and Mary washed the dishes, then went to the garden to gather crisp radishes and fresh peas for supper.

'Jeff dug the new potatoes before he went to work this morning,' Mary said. 'In summer we always leave them in the hill until we need them. They're so much more delicate in flavour when they're just out of the earth.'

On their way back from the garden they stopped at the root house for a jar of blueberries for a pie. Judy gasped when she saw the shelves filled with jams and jellies and canned fruit.

'I know it's so much more than Jeff and I need,' Mary said apologetically. 'But I love to gather berries, and any trip is much more fun when it has a reason. Jeff will enjoy the river more tomorrow because you want bear pictures. And picking berries is my weakness. I hate to pass them hanging on the bushes, begging to be gathered. It's hard to remember Jeff and I can only eat so many. Would you like wild blackcurrant jelly with your breakfast toast?'

'I'd love it,' Judy said. At Martha's Vineyard it had been considered a great delicacy, but Mary Baird had dozens of glasses.

'Then you must take some home with you,' she said, puting several glasses in the gaily woven Tlingit basket. 'And wild cranberries will be good with our venison tonight. I think that's everything we need.' She looked around a bit hopefully. 'Unless you see something— Oh, yes! I know you'll like this wild strawberry preserve.'

Judy agreed she would and smiled. If all this—peas and radishes and venison and jams and jellies—was living on the country, no one ever needed to feel sorry for the Bairds.

'But isn't it a lot of work?' she asked.

'It never seemed so,' Mary said, 'not when a country has been so good to us.'

They left their booty in the covered entry behind the kitchen and went to look at Vicky's cabin, nestling under a tall spruce.

'You mustn't feel you have to use it,' Mary Baird said. 'There are extra bedrooms in the house, but I thought you might like this.'

Judy was sure she'd like the cabin. She was already captivated by the little porch with a pole railing and a big chair for sunning. Mary opened the front door, and Judy gave a cry of delight.

The main room was lovely. Two cedar chests flanked the fireplace. They, the desk, the easy chair, even the bed with its four square posts, were evidently handmade, for she could see the little nibbles of the axe under the waxed surface. And they all were so simple and so exactly right for a log cabin. A small room beyond held a washstand, shelves, and hanging locker. A window looked out at the mountains, and the curtains were neither copper nor rose nor yet russet, but the warm chrysanthemum shades of autumn colouring, which brought out the glowing tones of the log walls.

'What a wonderful colour!' Judy said. 'And wherever did Vicky find it?'

'She dyed them. Three times—before she had just what she wanted. You like colour, don't you?'

'Yes. Colours can make me very happy—or awfully sad. How did you know?'

Mary Baird smiled. 'When Rod told me about your painting. People miss so much when they don't see colours, especially in Alaska. This was our first cabin while Jeff was building the house. Then it was Spence's when he and Vicky used to play at being Indians. And what a clutter! Fishlines of cedar root and basketmaking and even tubs of drying seaweed. Afterwards Vicky used it for a studio and made a darkroom. And now Jeff is already calling it young Jeff's cabin. I suppose it may be some day. Another boy playing at being an Indian!' She laughed gently. 'It makes one realize how fast the years go.'

'Wasn't it awfully hard to have Vicky go so far away?' Judy asked, and then was a bit shocked at her own temerity, but she'd wondered about this often. Rod had appeared to take New York and Greenwich Village for granted, but it must have seemed like the ends of the earth to Jeff and Mary.

'Hard?' Mary asked in a tone of surprise. 'I never thought of it that way. You don't—not when two people. . . . Why, Phil and Vicky just naturally belong together. I can't imagine one without the other.'

Judy's eyes widened. It wasn't at all the fairy story of the Prince Charming bearing Cinderella off from her life among the ashes. But she liked this version better. 'I see what you mean,' she said a little soberly. 'And it isn't as though you'd never see each other again. Rod told me they were coming home next summer.'

'Yes'—and Mary nodded happily—'when young Jeff is a bit older. Of course they can't stay long, but Jeff and I are old enough to travel and we've never been east of the Mississippi. Besides,' she added with a smile, 'Jeff has always liked to see new country.'

'And you'd love New York!' As she said it, Judy was surprised how certain she was about this.

'Do you think so?' Mary asked, looking pleased. 'The biggest city in the country or in the world except for London! I've never quite been able to imagine it, even from the photographs the children sent us. But most of all, I'd love to see Phil and Vicky in their home. And some day—perhaps we will.'

Judy knew she must be thinking of the years ahead when salmon traps would mean a greater ease in living, but it was the only reference she made to Tallac River all afternoon.

Nor did Jeff speak of it at supper except to say that Rod had stopped to tell him the run was over.

That evening as they planned the camera bear hunt, Judy knew she was in the hands of an expert, but it wasn't until the next day that she realized how much it meant to be with a man who could think as a bear thought. They went early in the morning when any self-respecting bear would still be catching his breakfast.

'Once they get their bellies filled, they're liable to be sleepin' in their wallows,' he said. 'And some of these old boys get hostile if you wake 'em sudden.'

Judy's spirits quailed a bit at the vision of a hostile brown bear, but she tried not to show it and apparently succeeded. At least Jeff seemed to have no misgivings about her courage when with lunch sacks tied to their belts, Jeff ahead with a rifle, they waded up the middle of the river. Judy, who had expected to be keyed up with the sense of danger, had instead an astonishing feeling of security. It wasn't the rifle, she decided, but Jeff, whose vigilance was so natural she was scarcely aware of it. They spoke in whispers, and then suddenly Jeff turned and motioned her to one side of an island. She followed him up the shelving rock, across the island, and to a high point where they peered over. Below them, not six feet away, a big, dark glistening bear sauntered along the shallow water, wholly unconscious of an audience. Judy aimed her camera, but Jeff motioned her to wait until the bear had passed beneath them. Then he nodded.

'He'd have heard the click,' he whispered. 'And right now he's got nothing on his mind but to enjoy hisself. I caught sight of his rump and figured he was heading for this island.'

Judy's fingers were trembling and seemed all thumbs as she snapped and snapped and turned the roll to get another, and another, and another.

'No need to hurry,' Jeff chuckled. 'He ain't looked over that pool yet. Watch this.'

The bear was contemplating it, and then his mind made up, he lay down on his back to loll in the refreshing stream. Judy was certain that if he'd had a sponge he would have washed his face. There was something so ludicrous about the look of fatuous delight on so huge a creature, with a head the size of a barrel, that they were both overcome with suppressed laughter. They watched him amble leisurely up the river to disappear around the bend.

'He's a big one,' Jeff said. 'Never saw him before. Must be a stranger, just moved in, but he's sure made hisself at home. Bet his hide would square better'n ten feet, and he'd weigh—well—close to thirteen hundred. I'd hate to pack that head and skin down a mountain. But you were lucky on your first bear.'

Judy looked at her camera wildly.

'Jeff,' she said in a tone of desolation. 'On those first pictures, when he was so close, I'm afraid I didn't set the shutter right. And if I didn't—' She stopped, unable to contemplate the awful possibility.

'You wouldn't be the first to freeze when you saw a brownie,' Jeff said. 'Once I spent three days getting a hunter from Chicago in shootin' distance from a beauty, and then he just waved his rifle at him. But that fellow turned out to be one of the finest sports I ever knew. And a good shot too. Took a fine skin home with him. So don't you worry. Plenty more bears up the river.'

'Jeff, you *are* nice!' she exclaimed. It had slipped out without thinking, and now she blushed. 'Not that I didn't —I mean, anyone else would have—'

'Liked it best the way you said it first.' Jeff grinned. 'And now let's get on up river.'

His promise of plenty of bears was more than fulfilled. Jeff knew each pool and usually what bears held fishing privileges, knew which bends demanded a cautious approach and those which had a screen of brush, knew too the very instant their subject felt its first instinctive sense of danger and when the huffing meant real truculence.

They lunched far up stream, sitting companionably on a point in a long open stretch of river, which Judy noticed with considerable relief had no heavy brush with low entrances to bear wallows. She was aware too that Jeff looked up and down river often while he told bear stories. Spence had shot his first bear at thirteen. 'But Vicky was a lot older when she got hers,' he said. 'Near sixteen. And she'd never shoot another.'

'How old was Rod when he got his?' she asked.

'He never got one. Never even wanted a rifle of his own. Which was funny too, because he's more Baird than the others.' He lighted his pipe and stared across the river. 'It took me a long time to figure that out,' he said.

Judy tightened. For a moment she feared Jeff intended to talk about Rod. Then he didn't, and somehow she felt he never would. She smiled at him. 'Have you always liked bears?' she asked.

'Liking isn't exactly it,' he said. 'Black bears, they don't count. But brownies and grizzlies—I respect them. Besides they were in the country long before me.'

10

ALL MORNING Rod had waited impatiently for the *Taku*, and when it finally arrived in early afternoon, he was on the float to meet it. Spence waved from the wheelhouse as he manoeuvred for a landing.

'Don't tie up,' Rod said. 'We're going over to see Daniels.'

'Fine. Hop aboard. Got all the dope with you?'

'Spawners count for the three summers, and our figures on the traps.' They had worked for hours on the estimates but as they crossed the bay, Rod said, 'Maybe we ought to raise the loan to more than three thousand a trap, Spence. Don't want to run short in case we strike a snag.'

'We've already allowed for that and we don't want to borrow more than we have to.'

'Daniels will be surprised we need so little. Bet he never put in a floating trap for twice as much.'

'The ones on Outer Point cost him plenty. He put those in the spring he chartered the *Taku*.'

'And he'll eat these up.' Rod's tone was jubilant. 'Next year the cannery's putting in another line. A three-line cannery! Biggest one around here!'

'Where'd you hear that?'

'From the engineer. That's why Jim Richards was up here on the *Chasima*. They've already leased the machinery.'

Spence looked at his brother. 'Gosh, that's good news! A three-line cannery is going to need a lot of fish. Couldn't be better timing.'

'That's what I thought.' Rod grinned. 'And the sooner Daniels hears about Tallac and knows he doesn't have to prospect new traps or order more purse seiners the more tickled he is going to be.'

They made the *Taku* fast, crossed the wharf, and entered the cannery. Rod paused a moment to watch the endless chain of fish move down the line toward the waiting cans.

It was all so familiar to him—the clatter of machinery, the slosh of water, and the oil-skinned workers.

They found Mr Daniels in his office. He seemed somewhat surprised at the visit but asked genially, 'And how are things with the Bairds?'

'Fine,' Spence said. 'Have you a little free time?'

The canner looked at his watch. 'I'm leaving on the *Dora* in an hour, but sit down and tell me what's on your mind.'

'We own two floating trap sites in Tallac Bay,' Rod began, 'and we need—'

'Tallac Bay? On Admiralty?' the canner asked in a tone of incredulity.

'Yes,' Rod said. 'And we came over—'

'You haven't paid the licence fees yet, have you?'

Rod nodded. 'They're in the names of—'

The canner turned to Spence. 'You should have talked to me before you wasted four hundred dollars. Why, I could have told you Tallac River was fished out long ago. Hasn't had a run for years.'

'It's had a run this summer,' Rod said.

'And what makes you think so?'

'I know the count of spawners.'

'Who took it?'

'Old Sha-goon-e-ish. He's been there all through the run.'

'An Indian! They'll tell you anything they think you'd like to hear. A few dozen fish and they'll make a good story of it.'

'I was there myself—counted spawners for three days, and I counted spawners the summer before and the year before that. Tallac River is coming back!' He said it proudly. 'It's going to be the same big salmon stream it was—'

'That old legend!' Daniels snorted. 'Heard it for years, ever since I came here, and I know how little there is in it. I've sent purse seiners to Tallac, and they didn't make enough money to pay for petrol, let alone the wages. I doubt if it ever was a salmon stream.'

'The poles from the big fishing camp are still standing,' Rod said.

'So are some of the weirs in your river at the head of Falcon Inlet. But you boys would think a man was crazy if he talked about a floating trap in Hidden Harbour. Sure, there's enough fish to feed a few Indians, but you know what a trap must catch to break even.'

'Traps at Tallac River would do better,' Rod said. 'I've got the figures on the runs for the last three years. I can show them to you.' He went on to tell the story of Tallac River, and because he felt the challenge in the canner's disbelief, he told it better than he ever had before. He knew he had to tell it well, and the warm glow in Spence's eyes reassured him. He told it with pride and with intensity. The restoration of a once rich salmon stream was something any man had a right to be proud of. 'Here are the records.' Rod laid them on the canner's desk. 'And just because nobody else cleared out a salmon stream, that doesn't prove it wouldn't work.'

'Nor that it would,' the canner snapped. 'So this was your idea! I might have guessed it!'

'And it was his money that paid for the dynamite and Sha-goon-e-ish's wages,' Spence said.

Mr Daniel's smile was bleak. 'I'm glad to hear that, Spence. Then you and Jeff are only stuck for the fees. Well, perhaps that's not too much to pay for a lesson in what wild-eyed ideas can cost you. These records'—and he thrust them aside with a disdainful pencil—'they don't mean anything. Any canner would tell you that.'

He got up from his chair and looked down at them. 'It takes more than one idea to stay in this business. We've lost our shirts finding that out—the hard way. Nobody knows why we have a good pack one season and barely break even the next three. It's happened often—happened to me on the mainland. Fish either come, or they don't, and there's nothing you, nor I, nor anyone else can do about it, except to set your traps where you have a chance. You ought to know that, Spence, from watching me prospect our sites. But there's one thing we are sure of. Salmon have been getting to their spawning grounds without any outside help since long before cans were invented. That we know.'

He turned to Rod. 'You might have had a run this year. And Tallac might have had runs in other years when nobody ran a tally count. But that doesn't make it a dependable salmon stream. And I wouldn't put a dollar of the company's money in that bay.'

He started for the door, then swung around.

'That doesn't mean, Spence, if you Bairds ever got a licence for a good site, I wouldn't be glad to loan the full cost of a trap.'

Rod and Spence watched him stride off to the cannery, then looked at each other. Neither spoke until they were aboard the *Taku*.

'Do you suppose it was my being on that pirate boat?' Rod asked. 'I always thought he had a hunch I was.'

'And if he did, he wouldn't turn down a chance to get fish. No canner would. It was only he didn't believe Tallac would have a run of pinks.'

Spence started the motor, and they crossed the bay, made the boat fast, and by a common impulse went into the cabin to sit in a stunned silence. Rod had been so sure, and now as he went over the interview trying to find where he'd made a mistake, he still couldn't quite credit the disaster. And it was disaster.

'Do you suppose if I'd had the sense to say it was your idea and you'd cleaned out the river, it would have made any difference?' Rod asked suddenly. 'It was ideas that got me fired from the cannery.'

'Daniels isn't turning down a chance to get fish just because you two had a run-in when you were a kid. And it wasn't the money. He took the trouble to make that clear. Of course, he knows he's already prospected every decent site around here.' Rod nodded. Spence was thinking aloud, going over the interview, step by step, just as he had. Then Spence added, 'It was because he doesn't believe you brought the pinks back!' There was an edge in his voice as he said it.

Rod stared at his brother. Spence was right. And if Spence's own faith was shaken, he couldn't blame him. All Spence had ever had to go on was what he'd told him.

Suddenly Spence got to his feet. 'Can you get Henry Dane to run the store tonight?'

'Sure,' Rod said, and waited.

'Matson and O'Brien are near enough to use Tallac pinks. Let's go down and talk to Jim Matson.'

'I'd thought of that,' Rod said. 'Only—' He didn't finish. Jim Matson was not the driving canner Daniels was, but a forlorn hope was better than none at all.

A half hour after Spence and Rod had left his office, Mr Daniels boarded the *Dora* to inspect the cannery's traps down the coast. As they pulled out from the wharf, he noticed the door of the store was closed and the *Taku* was still on the float. Ordinarily he wouldn't have been aware of this, for he made a conscious effort to remain aloof from Rampart Bay affairs. A cannery, run right, was all a man had time for, but this afternoon irritation had cut through his usual detachment. Even seeing the store was an annoying reminder of Rod's cocksureness. Then as the *Dora* was leaving the harbour, he looked back and saw that the *Taku* was getting under way. Now, of course, they were going to Hidden Harbour to report to Jeff that four hundred dollars in fees had been wasted. And he, through no fault of his own, would be regarded as the sole cause of their troubles.

'That crazy Baird kid!' he muttered to the skipper. 'Wonder if he'll ever get some sense.'

'Rod?' the skipper asked in surprise. 'Always struck me as a bright young fellow.'

'Too bright!' the canner growled. 'That's his trouble. Spence is worth a dozen of him, and so is Jeff.' For a moment he was tempted to share his sense of outrage, then decided to forget it. 'Keep along the west side,' he said. 'I promised Randolph I'd drop in Shaman Cove. We've got time this afternoon. I won't be more than half an hour.'

Judy and her father met him at the float.

'I'll tell Sang we have guests for supper,' David Randolph said.

'Sorry, but I'm on my way to a trap in Beaver Sound.'

'Then a drink, perhaps?'

'That would be fine. I've been promising myself a visit, but this is the first chance I've had.'

Mr Daniels admired the new house. 'Makes my quarters behind the office look pretty grim,' he said.

'But you're here only in the summer,' David Randolph said.

'And you're staying on?' the canner asked quickly.

'At least this winter. Perhaps longer. We're running into some interesting stuff.'

Mr Daniels raised his glass. 'Here's to more of it, and even better. That would be good news to have you as neighbours.' He turned to Judy. 'I was sorry Mrs Richards and Chris weren't aboard when the *Chasima* was in, but they may be up later. You and Chris would like each other.'

'I'd love to meet her,' Judy said. 'I've heard so much about how wonderful she was—' Then she suddenly remembered it was Rod who had said this about the evening she was aboard the *Taku* at the time of the shooting. She went on a bit hurriedly, 'Mrs Baird was talking of her last weekend when I was in Hidden Harbour and Jeff took me up the river to get bear pictures.'

'You were fortunate!' he said. 'Jeff must have liked you. He could be one of the most successful guides in brown bear country if he would take out big-game hunters. I've dug up several prospects for him, but—' He shrugged. 'Well, try to figure out Jeff Baird, or any of them for that matter.'

'I imagine nobody makes up Jeff's mind for him,' David Randolph observed mildly. 'One thing that most impressed me in him was—'

'That's what I thought until today!' the canner burst out in exasperation. 'I wouldn't have believed he or Spence would have fallen for a crazy idea of that kid, Rod. But they did! Spent four hundred dollars for two trap sites without even coming to talk to me—a man who's been in this game over twenty years and would have been only too glad to set them straight. Spence and Rod were in to see me just before I started down here. That's why I'm still boiling.

'Of course, it's none of my business. But I know where

that money came from. Out of Jeff's coffee can and Spence's savings towards another boat. But what does Rod care as long as he has a chance to show how smart he is. He had the nerve to tell me he'd brought salmon back on a river that never was any good in the first place. And expected me to believe it! I only hope Spence and Jeff have learned their lesson. Four hundred dollars wasted! And it needn't have happened to them.'

'But what would the Bairds want with trap sites?' David Randolph asked.

'That part of it made sense at least. Any canner will back an independent owner of a good site. The cost of building traps is beyond an ordinary fisherman, and a canner is glad to loan the money to make sure he'll get fish. I told Spence this afternoon I'd do the same for the Bairds any time they had a decent site. And I would. Making certain of a season's pack is a canner's headache. It's the difference between operating on a profit or a loss.'

'Then bringing a run of pinks back to a salmon stream is important to you, isn't it?' Judy asked. So far she had managed to remain silent, and now as Mr Daniels turned to stare in astonishment, she blushed. 'I thought that was what Rod told you he had done,' she said.

'Told me! Sure! And a cock-and-bull story about how he'd spent two years clearing out a river and had an Indian down there keeping tally on the spawners. Oh, I don't doubt but that he's done it. Probably read a book about the pink's two-year cycle and thought we old fellows never heard of it. But a little run in any stream doesn't mean a thing in the next year, or the year after or any year in the future. Not enough to spend over eight thousand dollars on two floating traps.'

'Do they cost that much?' her father asked, astonished. 'Just a frame of timbers to hang a bag of webbing from? At least'—and he smiled—'as I remember that's what you said they were. I've never seen one.'

'I was only trying to give you a general idea,' the canner said. 'But there's much more to them than that. The timbers must be very large, have floatability. We use spruce generally. Building the frame requires highly skilled labour. It must be mortised and bolted together so it will never rack in heavy gales or tides or currents and strong enough to support a bag of heavy wire webbing filled with twenty or thirty thousand salmon. Even the bag, as you call it, isn't as simple as it sounds. First there's a suspended wall of wire webbing to lead the fish into the enclosure, and this is divided so that eventually the fish go into the heart of the trap. The gear is costly—wire webbing, heavy anchors, thousands of feet of steel cable, and a brailing device with a power winch to raise the fish into the cannery tender. When you deal with fish in that number, you're way beyond man power.'

'I see,' David Randolph said. 'I can understand how all that runs into money!'

'About four thousand a trap in protected waters. Can run as high as ten in outside locations. But a good trap is more than worth it. Trap dreams are pretty heady, Randolph. It's not too many years ago since an independent owner sold his floating trap to a cannery for a hundred thousand dollars.'

'What!' David Randolph exclaimed. 'You really mean it?'

'Sure. That trap had caught a million fish every season.'

'At least the kid dreamed big.' David Randolph laughed, and then suddenly sobered. 'But that's the trouble with dreams. I'm afraid neither Spence nor Jeff could afford to lose four hundred dollars.'

'But they wouldn't have spent it if they hadn't believed in the river just as much as Rod did!' Judy burst out, and then as her father looked at her in surprise, she coloured. 'You know Jeff well enough, Dad, to know he wouldn't.'

'At least Spence should have known better,' Mr Daniels said. 'He was working for me the spring I laid out our traps, and he knows putting up a big pack of salmon is no child's play with easy answers out of a book. A canner who stays in this business has to learn to take big chances, bet a season's profit every summer, maybe lose his shirt, and try to make up his losses next year, guessing where the pinks will run. Sure, they go out to sea, but why a whole district will have good luck one year, and then two or three or even four of bad, no canner yet has found out. I haven't. And I've been through it—good luck and bad. I'm still guessing where they'll run. With salmon it could be anything—a storm at sea, wind, currents, where they come from, or only a quirk in a salmon's brain. I often wish those smart lads in Washington who write the bulletins would explain a few of those things to us old fellows.' He arose. 'Now I've got to run. Told the skipper I wouldn't be more than half an hour. I'm sorry I got started on the Bairds, but I feel better having blown off a bit, although I didn't come in for that. It just happened we were talking about Jeff. Only hope he doesn't take this too much to heart. Some day I'll try to explain it to him.'

The Randolphs went to the float to see Mr Daniels off and wave good-bye. At least David Randolph waved. Judy's gesture could hardly be considered a warm farewell.

'Nice chap, isn't he?' her father said as they walked back. 'Somehow I wouldn't have expected him to be so concerned. He never appeared to take much interest in Rampart Bay affairs.'

'No, he didn't,' she agreed in a toneless voice.

Her father looked at her sharply. 'Did you know about this river?'

'Of course! Rod told me. And I've been there and I saw the run. The salmon did come back! You should have heard Sha-goon-e-ish and his wife, Jennie, talking about how it would be like old times again when the Indians from this whole country depended on Tallac. I saw the poles and traces of the old clearing where they camped. There must have been hundreds of them! And now just because Mr Daniels didn't like Rod when he worked for him, he won't believe he's brought back a pink run.'

'You know better than to think that, Judy!'

'Why shouldn't I think it? The day we met him he said Rod had too many ideas. The trouble with Mr Daniels is he can't bear to have anyone differ with him, or even make a suggestion. How long would Alec have lasted if you'd acted that way?'

'Not very long, I'll admit,' her father said. 'But this

river is an entirely different matter. Daniels is a canner, and, Charlie Reynolds says, one of the best on this coast. He's built this cannery up from nothing. He may be a bit arbitrary, but he's earned the right to be. All he wants is fish, and if there'd been anything to Rod's idea, he wouldn't have hesitated a moment. He showed that very plainly. You're doing him an injustice.'

'And what's he done to Rod? And to the Bairds?'

'The four hundred dollars for licence fees is unfortunate. But that's not Daniels' fault. Rod shouldn't have rushed them into this scheme without consulting an experienced canner. Daniels would have been glad to help him. You'll have to admit, Judy, it was irresponsible behaviour. That's what really bothered Daniels.'

'But Rod couldn't have asked him! It had to be a secret until the run was over because Mr Daniels would have sent purse seiners to Tallac and caught the spawners before they ever reached the river. Then Rod could never have proved that he was right.'

'He hasn't proved anything yet, apparently.'

'But he has! You haven't even heard his story. And how can you know Daniels is so right about the river?'

'I don't know,' her father said. 'But it's reasonable to assume he knows more about the salmon industry than Rod. Aren't you being a bit absurd about this, Judy?'

'It's not absurd to resent the way he told the story! As though no one else had a right to think for himself. As though nothing new could be discovered! As though Rod didn't have proofs to offer! It's so autocratic—and so stupid —and so narrow-minded. I wish I'd told you about that river before he had a chance to.'

11

IT WAS DAYLIGHT the next morning before Spence and Rod were back in Rampart Bay, their last chance of a cannery loan gone completely. Jim Matson had scarcely listened to their story after he had heard Daniels had refused to risk money on Tallac River.

'That's good enough for me,' he said. 'Why don't you boys forget it?'

On their return trip neither spoke of the river, and when they'd made the *Taku* fast, Spence dived for the galley.

'What we need first is a pot of hot coffee,' he said. 'Be coming up in just a minute.'

Rod didn't even try to help as Spence sliced bread and brought out cups and saucers. Rod's thoughts were bitter. It was easy to say forget Tallac River, but he knew he couldn't.

'You can bet both Daniels and Matson will have purse seiners there next summer,' he said. 'Not a spawner will get upriver. All I did was give them another stream to strip. What do they care about a run two years after?' Then his voice quickened. 'But Matson believed a lot more than he admitted. Notice he took the trouble to tell us he'd buy fish from Tallac traps.'

'And so would Daniels,' Spence said.

He brought the coffee to the table. 'Throw that into you, feller, and let's get started for Hidden Harbour. Jeff and you and me have some figuring to do.'

'You mean—' Rod heard the sudden hope in his voice and broke off quickly. The licence fee, money Spence had been saving towards a boat, was bad enough. He had no right to let him in for any more.

'You didn't think I was quitting, did you?' Spence asked. Then he grinned and thrust out a hand.

Their clasp was like a pact between them. It didn't need words, and at that moment Rod couldn't have spoken. There was too big a lump in his throat as he thought that he should have known Spence better.

At Hidden Harbour they found Jeff and their mother eating breakfast. She baked more pancakes for her sons, and while she made trips from stove to table, they recounted their talks with Mr Daniels and Jim Matson. Jeff only listened and went on eating. When they'd finished the story, he pushed his plate back.

'Any reason I couldn't build those trap frames if I had a chance to study one a bit?' he asked. 'Nothin' but axe work to 'em is there?' Spence and Rod grinned at each other. It was so exactly the way Jeff would announce he hadn't given up. Now he looked at his two sons. 'Nothing Daniels or Matson said changed your minds, did it?'

'Not a bit,' Rod declared. 'But it's only fair to tell you that if—'

'This ain't no time to talk about the ifs!' Jeff snorted. 'Besides we done that once. Suppose you get out those figures you and Spence been working on. What does frame labour save you?'

'Plenty,' Spence said. 'Now we're licking two of the biggest items. Timber and labour. They alone would have cost a cannery two thousand easy.'

Jeff nodded. 'I already run a rough count of spruce on my timber claim, so we know we ain't going to have to buy no trees. And I can build the frames at Rampart in that little cove beside the store.'

'And tow them down to Tallac with the sawmill tug,' Rod said.

'Hire the tug and a few men from the mill to help us haul and spot them,' Spence added. 'We'll have to find a man who knows how to hang the webbing. That's a tricky job, but with him to show us, we can do a lot of the work ourselves.' He began to write down new estimates beside the column of their old figures. 'Now we're getting somewhere!'

'What else you got on that list of yours?' Jeff asked.

Spence ran down the items. 'Heavy steel cable and big main anchors to hold the traps. That's going to hurt. Can't cut a cent off what we figured.' He looked around the circle. No one spoke. 'Then wire and cotton webbing. At least fifteen hundred for web alone besides all the other gear.' He read it off. 'Manila rope, light anchors to hold down the web. Heavy bolts to put the frames together and light steel cable for lashing. Tools. Floaters for the leads and a mooring scow besides.'

'Scratch out the scow,' Rod said. 'I can build it at the store this winter. Planking from the mill won't run high, and you can bet Tom Walsh will see I build it right. But the scow's winch is going to cost us plenty.'

'No sense in buying floaters,' Jeff said. 'I always reckoned those dead cedars would come in handy sometime. What's it figure up to?'

Spence added the new estimate, then rechecked it while they waited. 'Five thousand, two hundred dollars,' he said, 'for two traps.'

'And we were going to borrow six thousand dollars besides using our own savings!' Rod said.

The difference would come out of their own hides, but no one mentioned this.

'Five thousand, two hundred dollars, you say, Spence?' Jeff asked. 'Give us quite a piece to go.'

'I've got sixteen hundred savings,' Spence said. 'And a chance for a big towing job this fall, besides my freight line. But I have to get the *Taku*'s motor overhauled, especially if I'm going to run her ragged next winter.'

'The store's seven hundred ahead, and all the bills settled except for a payment on my motor boat,' Rod said. 'I'd have had that cleaned up, but I didn't want to keep Sha-goon-e-ish waiting for his wages. I ought to have a good fall season. A lot of trollers are moving in from outside, and if the kings hang on, I'll do all right.'

'Guess there's about four hundred in the coffee can, ain't there, Mary?' Jeff asked.

'Exactly four hundred and fifty-two dollars and sixty cents,' she said. 'I never knew you to come that close before.'

'And we won't need nothing this winter except a few

groceries,' Jeff said. 'Besides I ought to have a fair-sized jag of logs to sell by spring even with getting timbers and building traps. Keep me humping, but that never hurt a man. And if it looked like too close a squeak, I could even take a stranger on a bear hunt.'

Nothing Jeff could have said would have given greater proof of his determination. His wife gasped.

'But Jeff! Guiding just anyone wouldn't be like taking Phil's friends out to shoot a bear. No one could possibly be as nice as those two men.'

'Well, we ain't come to that pass yet, Mary,' Jeff said. 'What's our stakes add up to, Spence?'

'Twenty-seven hundred dollars. But remember more than traps come out of that—grub, gasoline, overhaul on the *Taku*, Rod's payment on his motor boat—and not even counting those things we're twenty-five hundred shy of what we need. We've got to have it by midwinter, making sure we can buy the gear before Jeff goes ahead to build the frames. And those traps have got to be built and spotted by the end of May.'

'We could be sure of building one trap,' Jeff began. 'Then take our time on the—'

'We'd lose that second licence unless we build both traps,' Rod said. 'It's the law.'

'Don't see no sense to that!' Jeff protested. 'What's their hurry if we aren't in one? Own both sites, don't we?'

'As long as we pay our yearly fees and have working traps, and there is sense to it, Jeff. They made the law read that way on purpose so canners couldn't take out licences for every site that had any chance at all and hold them for years.'

'Never thought of that, lad,' Jeff said, beginning to look very sober. 'And I suppose Daniels or Matson would get the other site.'

'One of them would be sure to,' Rod said.

'And we'd split the fish between us. That wouldn't be so bad, Rod. We could take our chances same as the other fellow does.'

'But we can't build up Tallac unless we can run it the

way we ought to!' Rod said. 'We've got to count the spawn-ers, make sure enough of them get upriver to keep it seeded. Rich and fertile, the way it used to be. In the beginning, we might have to close the traps even longer than the law says. Next year the run of pinks might not be worth two traps. It's the years after we have to think about.'

Suddenly his voice flattened as he realized what he was asking of the others. Spence and Jeff had already done more than their share, and he had no right to urge two traps upon them. 'Of course with one trap, we can be sure we'll get enough fish to pay for it even next year,' he went on. 'And the year after we'd have a big run. The other—' His eyes avoided theirs. 'It was only the way I was looking at it.'

'And the way to look at it,' Jeff said. 'I wasn't thinking what could happen to that river. It's got to be two traps. How about you, Spence?'

'Two traps or nothing,' Spence said.

'Looks like it's settled,' Jeff said. 'When you got to do a thing, you do it. It's sort of like—' and he chuckled— 'the way a fellow has to stop one of those big brownies when he's coming for him.'

Before the week was out, everyone in Rampart knew the Bairds intended to build two floating traps. There was some-thing about the story of Rod's secret clearing of a river, his two year wait for proof, Daniels' refusal to loan the money, and the Bairds' stubborn resolve to build their own traps that captured the imagination. No one could question Dan-iels' ability as a canner or judge the soundness of Rod's belief he had restored a salmon stream, but all Rampart shared the hope Rod was right. Even members of the can-nery crew found excuses for store errands to wish Rod well, while the trollers, to a man, were solidly behind him. Baird traps became the main subject of the evening talk, and fishermen made longer runs to tie up at Rod's float, as though their very presence testified their faith.

Charlie Reynolds made an effort to appear neutral. 'Funny thing about Daniels,' he remarked one day when he stopped in the store for a can of tobacco. 'You got to admire the way he built up this cannery. He's a driver, never let a bad year lick him, but he's an old-time canner, and they got their own ideas. Nothing will change them, but some day when we're running our own country, instead of the government in Washington, the salmon game might be a whole lot different.'

'If it isn't, there won't be any salmon,' Rod said tersely. He didn't want to talk about it especially. No fellow had a right to sound off until he'd really proved something. 'I was coming over this afternoon to get some lumber from you, Charlie.'

'For another card table and more benches? You're going to need 'em the way the trollers are piling in here. Bet they've already built more floating traps over pinochle than the Bairds could use in the whole of Alaska.'

Rod laughed. Charlie always blustered about things that had especially pleased him. 'I'm rigging up a bathhouse,' Rod explained. 'I can pipe the water from that hot spring up the slope right into a shack below. Give soap, a towel, and a hot bath for a quarter. Always intended to build one anyway and now—' He wanted to say it was little enough to show his appreciation, but he couldn't. 'Well, I'll have the only place on this island to use its warm springs and make it worth while for fellows to come in here. It will cost me hardly anything. Have everything I need except lumber for the tubs.'

'There's some odd pieces kicking around the mill I'd be glad to get rid of.' Charlie picked up his can of tobacco and prepared to leave. 'And you don't fool me none either, Rod. Why shouldn't they come in?'

'I couldn't run a store without them,' Rod began. 'And—'

'Yes. And you give 'em a place to hang out evenings, sell them good stuff, and don't gouge 'em on store prices either. I'll have those pieces waiting for you and don't try to pay me. And anything else you boys need for those traps goes on the books until next summer. That's what I came in to tell you.'

'Thank you, Charlie.' Rod had to say it, although he

knew the old mill owner hated to be thanked. 'But right now we've figured we could—'

'Figured!' Charlie snorted. 'What do I care how you figured! I'm telling you what I'm doing. Jumping Jehoshaphat! I'm a neighbour, ain't I? I bought the first log Jeff ever flung in water afore you were out of knee pants. Don't tell me how to run my business.'

He slammed the door behind him.

12

ROD WAS BECOMING increasingly aware of how long it had been since he'd last seen Judy, not since his talk with Daniels. He hadn't wanted to rush down with this news until he could tell her what the Bairds intended to do about the traps. He'd planned to tell her on last steamer day when he'd thought she would surely come to Rampart, but the strait had been so rough even the *Resolute* was rolling. Now he didn't want to wait until next mail day. The need to see her decided him to go to Shaman Cove that afternoon. He was hurrying through his store chores when, just before noon, he saw the *Working Stiff* enter the harbour.

The mine boat turned toward the cannery, and Rod saw Judy and her father cross the wharf and enter the office. Always before, they'd stopped at the store first, and he thought her father must be anxious to get off a cable and they'd be over soon. The noon whistle blew, and he told himself that naturally Daniels had asked them to stay for dinner. There was no reason for misgivings. As he ate his solitary lunch, he thought of Judy. This wasn't the way he'd planned to tell her about the Baird traps. Not after she'd talked to Daniels. She must be wondering why he hadn't gone to Shaman Cove and told her himself, might even be thinking those trap sites were as worthless as Daniels said they were. He couldn't blame her if she were. All she'd ever had was his version.

It was early afternoon before the *Working Stiff* came across the bay. Judy was alone. Rod went to the float to take the lines.

'Best landing you've ever made, and no audience,' he said, trying hard to sound casual.

'Aren't you one?' she asked, matching her tone to his. 'We talked so long at lunch Dad hadn't begun to write his letters, and the *Dora* is starting for Juneau in an hour. He didn't want to miss this chance to get mail off.' She seemed anxious that Rod should understand why her father wasn't with her. 'I brought Sang's grocery order. Poor man. He's out of eggs again.'

'And Daniels told you he wouldn't loan money for the traps,' Rod said.

'He told us that when he stopped off at the mine just after you and Spence had been in to see him. But I couldn't come on mail day. Alec wouldn't let me.'

'I should hope he wouldn't. The strait was smoking. And—you know, Judy,' he added as they walked up the ramp to the store, 'I was sort of glad you couldn't come.'

'Too down?' she asked.

'Not about Tallac! Because I didn't use my head and go to Matson in the first place. I ought to have known Daniels wouldn't let anybody tell him anything. He never has. But I was only thinking about how he was the biggest canner around here, with a third line next year, and would need fish. Be glad to hear of a new place to get them.'

'Would the other canner have loaned the money?'

'If he'd had first chance. Matson isn't the smart canner Daniels is, and I guess he knows it. That's why after Daniels turned us down he wouldn't—'

'So Mr Daniels is to blame for that too! I hope he's proud of what he's done!'

She sounded wrought up and angry. Rod remembered she'd seemed doubtful that Daniels would loan the money, and she'd been so right about it.

'Daniels didn't do that to us, Judy,' Rod said. 'I did it. I was so cocksure he'd believe my story. I ought to have figured it out better. I knew him. I was his time clerk once. I don't know why I thought he'd changed any. Now the Bairds have to build their own traps. That's what I let Jeff and Spence in for when we didn't go to Matson first. Shall we put up Sang's order now?'

'We'd better. Father wants to start home early.'

As they worked, he told her of the Bairds' breakfast-table conference on ways and means.

'Wish you could have been there, Judy. I never expected to hear Jeff calmly talking about raising five thousand dollars. But we can build both traps for little more than that and not owe a cent to any cannery. Got it figured down to the last foot of steel cable.'

'That's why it's so unfair of Mr Daniels to talk the way he does!' she burst out. 'Just because he didn't think of clearing that river doesn't prove it won't work! Or that the Bairds don't have the right to build their own traps! He wouldn't even listen when I tried to argue with him. Just sat there telling Dad what a foolish thing it was. And I knew, even before I had a chance to talk to you, that you people must know how you could do it. Why—why—it just didn't make sense you wouldn't!'

'I was hoping you'd feel that way about it, Judy.'

His hand found hers, and for a moment neither tried to put into words the sudden feeling of their closeness.

'It was all I could think of while I was waiting for you to come from the cannery,' Rod went on after a long silence. 'I was coming to see you this afternoon, and I'd have come long before this if I'd known Daniels had stopped there the day we saw him. I'm sorry, Judy, that he had to tell you first.'

'It was the way he told us! As though—as though the salmon run this summer hadn't proved a thing!'

'That's what he thinks.' He smiled at her. Always before he'd thought of her as a girl from outside. He'd never known this Judy, so hotly partisan and so refreshingly alive. Never had she been more attractive. He felt a little humble. 'I should have known you wouldn't believe Daniels, Judy,' he said.

'But he had no right to say such things before you even start to build your traps!'

'What's the difference? It isn't going to stop us.'

'But don't you see, Rod? He's an old canner, and people believe him. The idea of his telling Dad the Bairds didn't have a chance! It's so highhanded, as though his opinion was the only one that counted.'

Rod was suddenly very sober. 'Is that what stirred you up?'

'And why wouldn't it! Dad likes you Bairds, and I could see it bothered him.'

'But look, Judy, your father is a mining man, and he knows the risks people have to take. Gold is a bigger gamble than salmon any day. A vein can pinch out, but you have a chance to bring back pinks.'

'Yes,' she said. 'Dad does know—but—'

She didn't finish. He saw she was really troubled. He couldn't understand it but was sure she must be mistaken about her father.

'Any mining man knows enough about taking risks. I bet there's never been a mine started that everybody believed in.'

'This is different, Rod. Mr Daniels is a canner, and you're not! Oh, I wish I could have told Dad about the river, the way you told it to me. How you thought it out, and proved it. He'd have understood it then. He likes to see people use their minds, and he'd have known that Mr Daniels wasn't. But now—' Her eyes were desolate. 'Mr Daniels has spoiled the whole story.' She stood up. 'I have to go. I promised Dad we'd get home early.'

Neither Judy nor her father mentioned the Bairds until they were well out on the strait, but she could see he was concerned.

'I was sorry to hear about the Bairds,' he said. 'But Daniels is convinced they're actually going to build their own traps—or try to anyway. The money for the licence fees was bad enough. But two floating traps! It's incredible! Especially after two canners refused to spend a dollar on that river.'

'But that doesn't prove there wouldn't be salmon in it.'

'Two experienced men in the salmon industry?' he asked.

'And they'd both send purse seiners in there next summer and catch every fish before they even reached the river. That's why the Bairds have to build the traps.'

'Have to! Is that what Rod said? Doesn't he see what he's doing to his family? Before those traps are finished, if they ever are, the store and Spence's boat will be mortgaged and Jeff stripped of his savings. And for what? You have to respect the judgement of a man like Daniels. He knows the hazards of this game. That's all he was trying to save them.'

'But you don't understand what that river could mean to the Bairds. Or what Rod is trying to do! You've never listened to his story.'

'I've no doubt but that he thinks of it as a crusade of some sort. I've heard this talk about the restoration of a salmon stream. And who would be more eager to do a thing like that than Daniels with the biggest cannery in this district? Why, the man thinks salmon, dreams salmon! It's his whole life! If those traps were justifiable, he wouldn't hesitate a moment. And I don't like to see you make a martyred hero of a youthful visionary who is ready to sacrifice his family out of vanity and hurt pride.'

'That's what Mr Daniels wants to think! He's the one whose pride is hurt because Rod had an idea any canner should have had a long time ago, but he isn't honest enough to admit it. Rod has an idea, just like you have ideas about a mine or a prospect, and he has the same right to try to prove them. Jeff and Spence are just as anxious to build those traps as Rod is. And they believe the pink salmon are coming back to Tallac River.'

'They are hardly authorities on such a matter. Why didn't Rod tell Daniels about this while the run was on?'

'But he couldn't! It had to be a secret.'

'Isn't Rod being a bit melodramatic? Daniels would be the first to take an interest in this river and would back them. It isn't the money.'

'But the Bairds won't have to spend anywhere near what Mr Daniels said they would.' She was glad her father had given her an opportunity to explain this. 'They've thought of all sorts of ways to save. Jeff has the timber on his claim, and he's sure he can build the traps himself.'

'You mean Jeff intends to give up his own work? Not get logs into the water to send to market? Why, that's madness, Judy! He's spent years building up a way of life, and now that pair of fine people will be no better off than they were in the beginning. And all because of a boy's sense of self-importance.'

'It isn't self-importance.'

'You don't know that, Judy.'

'But I do! Rod told me all about the river, and how he happened to get to thinking about Tallac.'

Her father looked somewhat startled. 'I knew you'd seen quite a lot of him this summer, but I hadn't realized—' He broke off and stared across the channel for a moment. 'But if Rod did tell you, Judy, that doesn't mean—'

'He's honest, Dad! Terribly honest—even—even when he wouldn't have to be. It isn't the way you think it is at all. Tallac River is a chance they have to take. Everyone has to take a chance sometimes.'

There was a long silence.

'We don't have to take them, Judy,' he said at last, 'although it's often very tempting to make ourselves believe we do. But if a man must take a chance, he should be very sure the risk is all his own. As you know, I learned that all too well and too recently. I can't understand Rod's willingness to endanger the security of a whole family. Nor do I think you should applaud it because you've taken a dislike to Mr Daniels. That isn't logical, Judy. It isn't like you. That's all I was trying to say.'

In the next two weeks Judy and her father didn't mention Tallac River. But their talk on their way home from Rampart Bay troubled her. Of course she told herself it was the Lady Luck that had made her father feel as he did about Rod and his river, and he'd be the first to admit he'd been mistaken. No one was fairer than her father. And then she would wonder if Rod could possibly be wrong about his river. The thought slipped into her mind at odd moments despite her effort to shut it out. It was frightening, not only for Rod's sake, but for all the Bairds'.

She wished she could talk to Mary Baird, felt almost a compelling need to see her. There was something so steadfast about her. If Mary felt they must build the traps, it would justify the venture. But on Judy's trips to Rampart Bay, Jeff's sloop was never at the float.

'He's too busy slamming logs into water to spend time sailing to Rampart,' Rod explained the afternoon she found him working in the store, so intent he hadn't even heard her whistle.

'Not even on steamer day to get Vicky's letters?'

'I take their mail up. Saves Jeff a day and gives me a visit with them. Jeff's a wonder! Has a new idea about those traps every time I see him. They always ask when you're coming again. Mom said to tell you she hopes you will stay longer next time.'

'I'd love to,' she said. 'Hidden Harbour must be beautiful in September.'

'Finest month in the year. Jeff's already counting on another camera hunt. The bears have left the river, but he knows where you can see them. He likes you, Judy. A lot.'

She smiled with pleasure. 'I had a wonderful day with him. I—I thought—we got awfully well acquainted.'

'So did I, from some of the grand things he said about you. He had a fine time. He's missed Vicky and the jaunts they used to go on.'

To be even remotely considered as a substitute for a girl who must be an expert in woodcraft amazed her. 'But I was awful, Rod,' she confessed. 'I slipped on boulders and splashed water and frightened bears. And in the very best shot of all I froze and didn't get it.'

'That wasn't what I meant,' Rod said, and then abruptly changed the subject. 'Did Spence tell you he got that big towing job he was after?'

'I didn't see him the last time he came. He stopped only long enough to unload freight. Dad and I were disappointed. We'd thought of course he'd stay for supper.'

'He had to be thirty miles down the strait before the camp closed. Spence might as well throw his bed away. He won't have much use for it this fall. What do you think of my new counter?'

'Is that what you're building! I've been wondering. And why right in front of your kitchen doorway where you'll have to walk around it?'

'It's an eating place for trollers. They come in here tired and don't want to open cans and eat aboard their boats. I'm not much of a cook, but Henry Dane is always fussing around a kitchen. Doesn't even mind washing dishes. The food won't be fancy. Just a pot roast maybe. Steak, of course, on boat days. Henry's pies are wonderful. He's a lot better as a cook than he ever was as storekeeper.'

'And it would be the only restaurant on the strait,' she said.

'Sure! If a troller knew he could count on a warm supper, he wouldn't mind running a little farther. If it works out, I can turn it over to Henry. He's been wanting a job of his own, and I'll need him in the store while I help Jeff build the traps this winter.'

'Do you always plan everything so far ahead?' she asked suddenly.

'Playing it as close as we are, we have to.' He planed a rough spot on the counter's surface, then tested it thoughtfully with a finger. 'But if you mean like Spence does, I'm not so good. He's always known where he was headed.' He grinned at her. 'I'll have this eating counter going by next boat day. Will you come up and have the first meal with us?'

Judy laughed delightedly.

'Rod, I don't think anything would ever get you down.'

13

Judy didn't attend the opening of the restaurant.

On steamer day Alec announced at breakfast that it might be fit weather for trollers but nothing for a girl to be out in. 'Take a look with the glasses. Every sea is breaking.'

'But if the wind goes down by noon—' Judy began.

'It won't,' Alec said. 'It'll be blowing harder.'

'And Spence will bring the mail,' her father added. 'There's no special reason for your going.'

'Except I wanted to,' she said. Of course Rod wouldn't expect her to keep her promise, and a new eating place for trollers could hardly have been considered a notable event. But she had looked forward to it.

It was the first thing she asked about when she went to the float to meet the *Taku* the next morning.

'Every troller within forty miles must have been there,' Spence said. 'And you should have seen Henry! Prouder than he was about being made postmaster. No one had even guessed he could cook, and I don't know how Rod ever found it out. Wasn't a pie or a scrap of steak left when they closed the doors last night.'

He set the grocery order on the float for Sang, who was already on his way from the cook camp. 'Rod said to tell you he hid out a beef roast for you, but Henry beat him to all the steak.'

'Then it is a success,' she said.

'You'd think so if you saw that gang of trollers standing three-deep around the counter.'

'I knew it would be!'

'You did? And me—I tried to talk him out of it. Right now when we're already stretching as—'

'But it was the very time to do it!'

'The kid was right.' Spence put in his clutch, and the *Taku* began to draw away from the float. 'He generally is'— and he smiled at her—'and about everything he does.'

Judy laughed as she carried the mail sack to the cabin. Spence might have been referring to the store, but she suspected otherwise. At least it was gratifying to think that he approved of her. She sorted the letters. There were two from Aunt Nina, one for her and another for her father. She put his on the top of his mail on the desk, where he'd see it first, and went to her room to read her letters. She noticed her aunt's was very fat.

It began in Aunt Nina's usual brisk and newsy style. She'd closed the summer house at Martha's Vineyard. Judy found this somewhat startling but presumed she'd learn the reason for this unprecedented early departure somewhere in the letter. Cornelia Hamilton had been her guest. 'Cornelia, as you must remember, spent last winter in the Orient and said every moment of the tour was fascinating. Since then, of course, I've been reading Lafcadio Hearn again. I'd send a copy of his *Japanese Letters* to you, but I'm sure it wouldn't arrive before you left.' Judy frowned, reread the sentence to make certain this was what it actually said, then hurried on to the next paragraph.

'We couldn't have a better year to make the trip. You at loose ends, and practically at the doorway to the Orient. It's only a few days' voyage from Juneau to Seattle. So I felt safe engaging our passage on the *Mandalay*, leaving Seattle on September 28.' Judy looked quickly at a calendar. This was only ten days away. She gulped and went on with the letter. 'I particularly want to sail on her because the Aldriches will be aboard. Perhaps you don't remember Debbie. She is a few years older than you, but she's such a vital person— always in the centre of things. And any crossing is more pleasant when you have friends aboard.

'Isn't it lucky you are free to come this year? I've always wanted to visit the Orient, and since Cornelia's report I've been more determined than ever. And seeing it with you will be perfect. Aren't the place names enchanting? Yokohama, Peking, Shanghai, Hong Kong, Siam, Burma, Bali, and the Taj Mahal in India. Cornelia assures me we ought to spend at least six months, and even then we won't have seen half the places that we'd like to. Our first port will be

Yokohama, and after that I haven't let the travel agency put us on too fixed a schedule. We'll find our own adventures. There are so many possibilities, and they are so irresistible it's hard to choose, but I'm making a list of some places I'm sure we must see. Show it to David for his opinion in case he absolutely refuses to see us off.'

Judy read the next few pages, her thoughts whirling. She had not yet recovered when her father appeared with his letter from Aunt Nina in one hand and a steamship schedule in the other.

'Isn't this wonderful, Judy?' he demanded. 'A whole winter in the Orient. It's ten years since I've been there, but I've never forgotten it.'

'But rushing off so! Closing her house at Martha's Vineyard early! Making reservations before she even asked me! It's so different from anything she's ever done before! Why, two years ago when we went to Europe, she had everything planned for months! And this sailing on a special ship just because people she knows will be aboard!'

'Probably trying to give you a pleasant crossing. But, Judy, we haven't time for all this now.' He turned to the steamship schedule. 'We can catch the *Queen* at Juneau on Tuesday and be in Seattle the morning of the twenty-sixth. That gives us—'

'You mean you'll see us off!'

'Of course,' he said, 'and then go on to California for a conference with the company. I'll have to get some letters and cables off. Will you tell Alec I want him to go to Juneau.'

'But I can take them to Rampart Bay,' she said.

'I want them to go tonight, so I'll have answers waiting for me when we take the *Queen*. I'll cable Nina we'll meet her at her hotel as she suggested. I'll have the letters written in an hour. If Alec goes this morning, he can be back here late tomorrow night. I'm going to need him in the next few days.' Judy started for the door. 'Tell Alec to take Harry along,' he called after her, 'and get those compressor parts repaired in case we have another breakdown.'

Until the *Working Stiff* departed, Judy was too busy helping stow the boat with food and blankets to realize what it was all about. Everything had been settled so quickly. Even when the cables were finally on their way, the thought of a winter in the Orient still seemed somehow very unreal.

It was afternoon before she had an opportunity to reread Aunt Nina's letter and realize she was actually going away, would be gone for half a year, perhaps longer. It would be spring before she could possibly be back in Alaska. She looked out at the mountains and felt a little stab of anguish at this sudden parting. A whole winter in the Orient was different than just a visit in Boston. There would be an ocean between, and a fixed plan of travel. There was something so definite about it. Letters from Rod would be so few and take so long to reach her. She wouldn't know if the Bairds had built their traps or have any sense of sharing in their triumph.

The realization of this came as a sudden wrench, and it sharpened her first impression of something inexplicable about the letter. Aunt Nina might condone the unexpected in others, but she herself never acted on a sudden impulse. Nor did she ever coerce another. Yet the letter verged on this. At least it left no loophole for refusal. But her recent letters had approved of Judy's decision to stay on for a long visit with her father, and she hadn't even pressed for a definite date when she might expect Judy to come to Boston.

Judy remembered the winter Natalie Dean had been rushed off to Europe because she professed to have a crush on her music teacher. He was a little mouse of a man, and no one had believed it except Natalie's parents, who didn't realize their daughter's leaning toward the dramatic. It didn't seem possible Aunt Nina had taken recourse to that ancient solution for what her generation sometimes referred to as a 'difficult situation'. Surely she couldn't have believed a mining camp in Alaska warranted such drastic measures unless—and Judy straightened with a jerk—unless her father had written something to upset Aunt Nina.

Of course, that must be it! Judy recalled now that her father hadn't even asked if she wanted to spend a winter in the Orient, only assumed that she did, and rushed Alec off to Juneau with the cables. If he had appealed to his sister for help, she would have dashed to the rescue, and being Aunt Nina, she'd be terribly efficient. Perhaps she didn't even want to go to the Orient, but wild horses could never drag this admission from her.

Judy put away the letter. It all fitted together so beautifully. Even if she'd said she didn't want to go, as she almost had before she'd realized she couldn't refuse Aunt Nina, she would have had to go anyway. She knew this now. You had to do things other people expected of you unless you had a definite reason for refusing. And she didn't. Only a strange reluctance, and a feeling too of resentment. It had bothered her when she read the letter, and it bothered her even more now that she understood it. Outsiders had no right to crowd in until—until she'd had a chance to know Rod better, and it came to her with a shock that Aunt Nina and her father weren't outsiders. Yet they were really, she thought. But when your family didn't know this, there was nothing you could do about it.

That evening her father read Aunt Nina's lengthy letter. He studied the proposed itinerary with approval.

'A few places I'd cross off and some I'd add,' he said. 'We'll take my old maps and notes along on the _Queen_ and work out side trips. But this has all the earmarks of a grand winter for you girls, and, as Nina says, this is the year to go. You have been at sort of loose ends, Judy.'

'Did you write and tell her that?' Judy asked.

He looked up, startled. 'Well—I did admit I agreed with her that a mining camp had nothing to offer a girl your age —or any other age, for that matter.'

'But she knew I was going east for a visit later!'

'A visit, yes! But a whole winter in the Orient, Judy! Think what that will mean! And you need it, Judy. At seventeen your world should be opening up, giving you new vistas, fresh experiences—not growing narrow. That's all I wrote Nina when I tried to give her a picture of what your life is here. Miners and fishermen. The only community is Rampart Bay with a sawmill, a cannery, and a store, and this winter, when the cannery is closed, there won't be more than a dozen people. No female less than fifty. No young people except the Baird boys.'

'I see,' she said. She could imagine Aunt Nina's thoughts when she read the letter.

'It's all too tight, too narrow, too ingrown, Judy! Life shuts in around you, gets out of all proportion. Small things become important. They're bound to, Judy. You can't help it. Like the way you were stirred up about that river and so illogical you were hardly civil to poor old Daniels because he stuck to facts. I was sorry to see—'

'And then you sent Aunt Nina a cable,' she said.

'Yes, I did. Because it was all my fault really. If it hadn't been for the Lady Luck, you would never have come here in the first place. Your summer would have been different— full of stimulating new encounters. You're still questing, trying to find yourself. I was at your age. It's only natural. And this winter you will get a broader outlook. You can't help but do it, Judy, and then next summer when you come back here, it will be a fresh adventure.' He stood up and smiled at her. 'I'm sure of this. And now I have some big days ahead. We'll have to leave for Juneau on Monday. The *Queen* sails early the next morning.'

Judy went to her room, although she wasn't sleepy. She wanted time to think. So it had been Rod and Tallac River after all! Her father hadn't said it was Rod especially. But he hadn't dismissed him or his achievement quite so lightly as he appeared to. Visionary and irresponsible, and even a threat to the security of others, as her father thought him, he had given Rod an importance she hadn't expected. Surprising as this was, she found it strangely gratifying. Rod was a person anyone would be aware of.

All next day Judy watched the entrance, hoping to see Rod's boat. There was no special reason for his coming, but he might. This was Friday, and even if the *Working Stiff* came home that night, only two days were left for a trip to Rampart Bay. If Alec were delayed or the strait too rough, she might not be able to go tomorrow. But she couldn't leave Alaska without saying good-bye to Rod.

At midnight she heard the *Working Stiff* arrive. Next morning she departed early. She'd never seen the strait more lovely. A fresh breeze ruffled the water, and the sea was sheathed in silver. Her favourite mountain lay just ahead, climbing from the sea in great granite steps. She had a poignant feeling of farewell and tried to fix the mountain's beauty in her mind, to carry the memory of it with her. She hadn't realized she'd put her roots down quite so deeply, and now she suddenly wondered why she'd ever been a little proud of not belonging anywhere in particular.

It was mid-morning when she turned into Rampart Bay. Rod came out of the freight shed and took the lines.

'I was hoping a day like this would bring you,' he said. 'I'd have been down yesterday, but I had to work on the pipeline from the hot spring.'

'Have you finished?' Judy asked. 'Because I've never seen a hot spring.'

'Come see one now,' he said. 'I have to replace a plank in the dam.'

They climbed the slope to a bench above the beach, where hot water bubbled up in a great black pool and over-flowed in a little brook. Rod had built a dam to hold the water.

'Got my own pressure system,' he said.

Judy stared into the dark depths, where water rushed out from between the rocks. There was something eerie in this proof of the intense heat so near the surface of the earth.

'How hot is it?' she asked curiously.

'Don't put your hand in it,' he warned. 'Won't take me a minute to replace this plank. You're not in a hurry, are you?'

She said she wasn't and sat on a boulder to look out over the harbour. From up here it was so different. She hadn't known the bay was so beautiful with a rim of mountains around it. Rod finished his work and stretched out on the ground beside her.

'I'm glad we came up here today,' she said. 'I might have missed knowing how really lovely this harbour is. I would have remembered it only as I saw it from the water.'

She was thinking how many things she must have missed when she realized he was staring at her. Naturally he hadn't understood. 'I didn't tell you,' she said, 'but I'm going away on Monday.'

'Don't go, Judy!' The words burst from him.

'I have to, Rod. It's all arranged. Dad has already sent a cable that we would meet Aunt Nina in Seattle. We're going on the *Queen* next Tuesday.'

'And then?' he asked quietly. He was tracing little patterns on the earth, and he didn't look at her.

'We're going to the Orient for—for the winter. I didn't know about it until Aunt Nina wrote that she'd already made our reservations.' There was a plea in her voice that he understand this. 'Spence brought her letter last mail day.'

He looked up. 'I've always known you'd have to go sometime. You told me when you first came up here. But—I—I guess I didn't let myself think about it.' His smile was a bit crooked. 'Somehow it seemed easier—not to.'

'But I'm coming back,' she said. 'We'll only be away about six months.'

'Only!' It made it sound like an eternity. He stared out over the harbour. 'Don't you see, Judy? In six months—you away and me here—so much can happen. That's what got me! I'm sorry.' He shrugged. 'Coming so suddenly. It would have been different if—if I'd been expecting it. But half a year, Judy!'

She knew what he meant. And separations did change people's feelings. It wasn't anything so simple as forgetting, but other things got between. It was what her father had been saying when he told her she'd come back with a fresh outlook. And perhaps Rod would have one too.

'I know you have to go, Judy,' Rod said after a long silence. 'But it'll be awfully empty around here. You know that, don't you? And you know how I feel about you? I knew it a long time ago.'

She had known how he felt, she thought, known it without letting herself realize she knew it. She hadn't wanted to make anything special of their instant liking for each other, of that natural sense of fellowship. It had grown up so easily, without having to be put into words or even into thoughts. And now, except for her father and Aunt Nina and her having to go away, this never would have happened.

'You did know, didn't you, Judy?' he asked again.

She nodded wordlessly.

'And if you didn't come back—' he began.

'But I will!'

'Promise?'

'It's more than just a promise,' she said gravely. 'I couldn't not come, Rod.' She was certain of this. The discovery was still so new she found it difficult to explain even to herself. It wasn't Alaska, or the river. It was Rod, and what he might mean.

He caught her to him. 'That's all I ask. Oh, Judy, if you only knew how much you've meant! All the things I've planned to do and what I want to be. For you, Judy, so— you could feel all right about us. I haven't talked about it. Right now, there isn't much use in talking. But I want you to know I've thought about it. And when you come back, we'll have the traps built and I''ll have a chance to prove something. I know what Daniels thinks about me. Just a kid who doesn't care what he does to his family. And, of course, your father must believe him. But you didn't, Judy!'

'No,' she said. 'I couldn't, Rod. I knew different. And Dad will too when he really understands. It's only now when—' She stopped. There was no need to talk about it. Rod hadn't let this touch him. She smiled up at him. 'Did anybody ever tell you how much you are like Jeff?' she asked.

He laughed, and there was a ring of happiness in his laughter. 'Jeff has—and now you,' he said. 'Will you write to me, Judy?'

'From our first port in Japan. And then I'll tell you where to send your letters.'

14

It was November when Rod received Judy's first letter, mailed in Tokyo. Spence had already reported that David Randolph had returned to Shaman Cove after seeing Judy and her aunt off on the *Mandalay*.

'Must be quite a ship,' Spence had said. 'And that's a real trip they're taking. Mr Randolph said he didn't expect Judy back before next summer.' He glanced briefly in Rod's direction. 'But she'd told me she'd only be away six months.'

'The Orient is a lot of country,' Rod said.

He didn't want even Spence to guess what Judy's going had done to him or how much he missed her. This was Judy's and his affair. Afterwards, however, when he followed her itinerary on an atlas, he was glad Spence had prepared him for the longer separation. In the first three months, they weren't going to cover much ground. At that rate, it would be summer before Judy returned.

'As soon as Aunt Nina has decided where we'll be after the Christmas holidays, I'll let you know,' she wrote. 'Letters take so long. I'll be lucky if I hear from you before December, but I'll leave our forwarding address everywhere I go. So be sure and write to me at Singapore and Bangkok.' She told him she had shopped in Tokyo, and the shops were fascinating. She'd sent his mother a little gift, a mandarin coat, just to say how often she thought about her lovely weekend at Hidden Harbour. 'The minute I saw it, I knew how wonderful she would look in it. Tell her if she doesn't like it she mustn't think she has to wear it. And write me all the news. Everything. Especially about the traps and whether Jeff has already begun to build them. What an exciting day that will be! I wish so often I could be there to share it.

With love, Judy.'

Rod smiled wryly as he folded the letter. There was so little news to send, at least the kind he'd like to write. Their savings hadn't climbed as they had hoped. The overhaul of the *Taku*'s motor had been a blow. Spence and Tom Walsh had found two cracked cylinders when they dismantled.

'Buying new ones and Tom's wages will take a chunk out of my sixteen hundred,' Spence said. 'But I've got to do it, Rod.'

'Sure you have to,' Rod agreed. 'We always knew we'd run into bad luck somewhere, and it's better to get it behind us early.'

He hoped it was behind them. He'd made the last payment on his motor boat and begun to build the scow. The slack season in the store had started. Many trollers had laid off for the winter, but the ones who remained were loyal Baird men, and now, with sunset at four o'clock and long dark evenings, the pinochle table, the hot baths, and the chance for a good supper had made Rampart Bay a troller's club. Even more important, Henry Dane, having discovered the heady brew of applause, had bloomed. Not only was he a cook but a willing postmaster and a genuinely liked clerk.

Rod reported only the cheerful news in the letters he sent Judy at both Singapore and Bangkok. Jeff would not begin to build the traps until late winter, but he'd already cut the timbers. 'The best timbers to ever go into a trap in southeastern Alaska,' Rod said, but he didn't add that all these preparations would be wasted if they failed to raise the money to buy equipment.

They had so far to go, and so little time. Store and freighting profits couldn't possibly add up to twenty-five hundred dollars in the next few months. He'd spent his evenings covering sheets of paper with long columns of figures. Apparently Spence had been doing the same thing, for he stopped at the store one afternoon.

'If we raised a thousand dollars, we could earn the rest,' he said. 'Let's take a trip to Juneau.'

For a moment Rod didn't answer. That Spence, to whom debt was abhorrent, had suggested this only proved how desperate their situation was. 'This is different from asking a canner to back a trap for the sake of getting fish,' he said. 'Are you thinking of banks?'

'Or anyone else who'll loan the money. We've got to make sure of webbing, cable, and all the other gear before Jeff starts to build trap frames. That only gives us till February, at the latest. You have all the trollers you can count on for the winter. The *Taku* can't do any better than she's doing now. That towing job wasn't as big as I'd counted on, and the new cylinders set us back a lot.'

They were at a Juneau bank when it opened the next morning. The president listened to their story.

'I never heard of a canner who wouldn't loan money on a good trap prospect,' he said. 'Daniels is adding another line for spring, and he isn't overlooking a chance for fish. If he says "No" to this river of yours, what do you expect me to say?'

They spent the day applying to banks, wholesale houses, anyone who might loan money. Everyone took the same view. They were back at Rampart Bay the following afternoon.

'Which puts it all up to us,' Rod said when they made fast at the home float. 'If I'd only used my head and gone to Jim Matson in the first place, we wouldn't be in this spot. And now that third line of Daniels has only made it harder for us.'

'And hungrier for fish next summer,' Spence said with a grin. It was heartening, but no answer to how they would raise a thousand dollars to bring them within striking distance of their goal.

'I can put a mortgage on the *Taku*,' Spence said after a moment.

'It hasn't come to that yet!' Rod declared vehemently. He knew what that offer had cost Spence. 'And it never will, if I can help it. There's bound to be some way to get the money.'

Spence nodded, and then he laughed. 'I'll take back one thing I said, Rod. Remember how I told you Tallac Bay was made to order for us? Right now it doesn't look as though it was. Next time you fix up a bay, you make it smaller so there isn't room for more than one trap.'

'There won't be a next time if we run that river ourselves, and like it ought to be. And we're going to, Spence.'

He sounded confident, but as the days slipped by, Rod was finding it harder and harder to write the weekly letter to Judy. He didn't tell her much about the traps, but instead filled them with Rampart Bay news. In mid-December he wrote of Christmas plans and presents waiting for her. He'd asked Jennie to weave an enormous basket with a cover and insisted there must be lots of yellow in it so it would look well in her room. The famous old-time weaver had made a beauty, and Sha-goon-e-ish had done a carving. 'It's a brown bear,' he explained. 'I hope you'll like it. He wanted to do a big ceremonial seal feast dish, but I didn't see where you could put it in your place at Shaman Cove. Charlie Reynolds is going to give his usual Christmas party at the mill. Wouldn't it be grand if you could be there! I can't tell you how much I miss you, Judy.'

Afterwards, when the letter had gone off on the *Resolute*, he thought perhaps he should have answered her questions about the traps, but he hadn't wanted her to know they were worried. Yet she would know anyway. She had a way of always knowing how the other fellow felt.

Then, a few evenings later, Rod wondered if he had possibly found the answer, and when he least expected to, while he was watching the evening pinochle game.

As Ed Erickson dealt the sixty-four card pack he looked across the table. 'Didn't you tell me, Pete, that your brother was trying to find a purse seiner? Think I know where he can get one cheap.'

Pete picked up his hand, waited until Ed had turned the trump, then asked, 'Where? And how cheap?'

'At Hot Water Cove. The cannery's folding up. Price ought to be right. They must be in real trouble, throwing in the sponge this early.'

'Who'd my brother see?' Pete asked. 'The watchman?'

'Owner's watching it himself to save wages. Kennedy's his name.'

'What else has he got to sell?' Rod asked quickly.

'I don't know. Purse seiner's all this fellow told me about,' Ed said.

Rod walked away. He had thought of trying to buy secondhand gear, but usually they only knew a cannery was folding when it didn't open in the spring. And this would be too late to save them.

Hot Water Cove was two days' run from Rampart Bay. Rod started for it at daylight the next morning.

Five days later he was back in Rampart Bay. The *Taku* was at the float. Spence stuck his head out the wheelhouse door.

'Where the heck have you been for a week?' he demanded.

Rod grinned. 'Getting the thousand dollars, and more besides. Don't have to pay any interest or even give it back. Wait a minute till I come aboard.'

Spence was waiting for him in the wheelhouse.

'Got 8,000 feet of steel cable, heavy anchors, and a winch for the mooring scow, all just one year old, and for half price,' Rod said. 'Eleven hundred dollars. Paid the fellow half down and told him he'd have the rest when we came with the scow to get the stuff. It's up the coast in Hot Water Cove.'

Spence let out a war whoop. 'That does it, kid! But how'd it happen? All Henry could tell us was you'd be away for a few days. I was getting steamed up about you.'

Rod told the story. 'Figured Kennedy might have a trap or two. It was worth finding out anyway.'

'It saved our necks. Nothing can stop us now. Wait till Jeff hears. I bet he's been doing a little figuring on his own. Guess we all have, and not liking to admit it.'

It was as close as any of them had come to acknowledging the threat of failure. That evening Rod wrote a long letter to Judy, the first letter to her he had really enjoyed writing. Now he could honestly say they would build the traps in early March, have them in Tallac Bay by the end of April.

Rod rushed to finish the mooring scow, and a week later the big heavy craft was pushed down the skids. Then he and Spence towed the scow to Hot Water Cove, where Spence installed the winch so they would be able to lift anchors and heavy cable to the shore in Tallac Bay to be ready for the traps. This was luck they hadn't even hoped for.

Early in March Jeff and Mary came from Hidden Harbour to live with Rod while he and Jeff built the trap frames. It was hard and slow work. Each great log had to be cut and fitted, mortised at the ends, holes bored through by hand, heavy bolts driven through to hold the logs together, and then each joint wound with heavy steel cable. But gradually the big rectangles, 100 by 40 feet, began to take shape. And when these were complete, the rectangles had to be divided into three compartments with other logs. All this was toil, heavy toil, often a real hardship. Rod and Jeff began work before daylight and finished long after dark. The water was icy, the wind chilling. Sometimes snow fell. But they ignored discomfort and numbing cold. Jeff had always been a driving, intense worker. Now he brought a new quality to his attack. His spirit was a mixture of savagery and exultation.

The building of the frames became a sort of drama for the community at large, and a matter of pride too. No one would have dared to suggest to any of the trollers that those frames wouldn't survive tide and currents of even a North Pacific gale. They recognized a master craftsman, and they paid him homage. 'Honest solid,' Jeff called the frames when they were finished, and he said it proudly.

'And now your ma and I can go back to Hidden Harbour,' Jeff announced at supper.

Rod looked up in surprise. 'Aren't you staying long enough to see them towed away? I thought you'd come with us.'

'Right now I'd like to fling a few logs into the salt chuck,' Jeff said. 'And your ma has things she'd like to do. Ain't you, Mary?'

She smiled. 'We both want to see our home, Rod,' she said. 'We've never been away so long since we came to Alaska. It's been wonderful, though. I'll miss the store and the trollers and Henry's cooking.'

'When you're ready to rig the webbing, we'll be back to help,' Jeff said.

The wire and cotton webbing had arrived in early April, and the huge rolls, stored in the freight shed, brought a sense of triumph. They were the last big outlay, and the Bairds still had money enough to pay for the sawmill tug and a crew to string the webbing. But that was all. They had reached the bottom of their savings.

Next morning Rod saw Jeff and Mary off, then went to the sawmill.

'See your traps are finished,' Charlie Reynolds said. 'But I knew Jeff could do it. Better axeman never lived. And I've been thinking about that towing job. This ain't going to be like moving a jag of logs.'

'But we'll have the *Taku* and my motor boat besides,' Rod said.

'Oh, I don't doubt but the three of us could tow one. But how fast can we tow it? We got to make Tallac Bay in one ebb tide. If we didn't, and the strait got rough when the flood started, we'd have a hard time getting that trap into shelter. That's what's worrying me.'

It was worrying Rod too, but he didn't admit it. Now, at the end of their resources, they had to use the sawmill tug. If they chartered a big tug from Juneau and it was held up by weather, the cost for two traps might run into hundreds of dollars.

'If we had a strong ebb,' Rod said, 'and got under way before the change of tide so we'd be out on the strait by the beginning, we could ride it all the way to Tallac Bay. That's how Spence figured, and he's worked tides ever since he owned the *Taku*. There's a good ebb tomorrow night.'

Charlie considered for a moment. 'We can try it. But we'll have to buck the last of the flood getting out of the harbour.'

Next evening after supper they made the sawmill tug fast to a trap and strung the *Taku* and Rod's motor boat in the lead. All the trollers were on the float to watch the departure. Throttles open, the three boats pulled against the flood. They pulled for an hour and hadn't made the entrance of the harbour. It was folly to even try the straits.

'It's like being hooked on to an island!' Charlie said. 'We

got to work out some other way. Maybe in two ebbs we could make it.'

Rod doubted this, but he didn't say so.

'Tell you what,' Spence said. 'We'll moor the trap to the beach. I've got to make my freight run, but I'll make it in a hurry and be back here in a couple of days. Then we'll figure out a new scheme.'

A few of the trollers were still standing on the float when Rod returned.

'It'll take a lot more power to handle that job,' one remarked.

Rod agreed, but he didn't want to talk about it then. He went to bed but didn't sleep well, and the next morning the outlook seemed as black as ever. He wished Spence was there to talk it over. If they tried Charlie's scheme of a layover between the ebbs, it would take two or three days to move each trap, and naturally they'd want to pay for all that extra time. On the other hand there was no knowing what a big tug from Juneau would cost. Either scheme would run far more than they had planned. It would be money they didn't have. Yet the traps must be towed to Tallac Bay somehow. After months of work the one thing they'd taken for granted had gone wrong. They should have realized how unwieldy a big trap was, and hindsight added to Rod's chagrin.

That evening he was surprised when the trollers didn't linger in the store. A few ate a hurried supper and departed. By dark the last of them were gone and Henry had finished in the kitchen. Rod was alone when Ed Erickson came back to the store. He stood in the doorway.

'There's twenty-six of us here tonight besides Charlie's tug and your motor boat,' he said. 'The lot of us can out-tow any tug in Juneau. Come on and get your lines on her.'

He disappeared into the darkness.

Trolling boat engines were barking into life. Men were shouting to each other. Suddenly the bay was filled with green, red, and white running lights. Rod ran to his motor boat and followed the others. When he reached the trap, boats were already making fast. Rod jumped out on a timber and discovered he had nothing to do but make a hitch with his line. This was no spontaneous affair. It had been well planned. Trolling boats were in formation, longer lines ran to a second row in front. Charlie Reynolds was fastening a cable from his tug.

'You start this, Charlie?' Rod asked.

'No. It's just those hot baths and pinochle games and fair prices coming back on the tide,' he said. 'Sometimes, Rod, it pays to be decent.'

A troller in the lead sounded three sharp blasts on his whistle. Rod leaped into his boat and threw in the clutch. He looked back at the cliff above the trap. It began to recede, slowly at first, then faster.

'Look at her walk!' a troller shouted from a nearby boat.

Water gurgled around the timbers. A few minutes later they were out of the harbour. Later, on the strait, a big tide was gathering headway. The trollers lashed their boats together in groups of three and four so one could steer while the others slept. At dawn the trap was fast to the beach in Tallac Bay and the trollers had dispersed for the day's work.

Next night they took the second trap. Rod wanted to fill their tanks with free petrol, but they wouldn't listen to him. As on the first night, they went about the business of fastening on and towing, even mooring the trap to shore in early daylight, as though all this was none of Rod's affair. They avoided him as much as possible, never gave him a chance to make a decent speech, and would have jeered if he'd tried to make one. But he knew he would never forget the warmth and the elation that the friendship of these lone wanderers of northern seas had brought him. He didn't try to thank them. He just let it drop.

That evening when he wrote Judy a long letter about the towing, he thought how she would have loved to have seen it, to have shared it with him. More than anyone he'd ever known, she would understand how much it meant. As he addressed the envelope, he realized this would be the last letter that must cross the Pacific. Judy would be in San Francisco in early May. 'But not in Alaska,' she had written. 'Aunt Nina wants to see California, and wants me with her. We're going to a house party at Lake Tahoe, and another at Pebble Beach. But I'll surely be home the first week in June.'

Now with the traps safe in Tallac Bay, the Bairds were over the last hump, ready to hang the webbing. Rod had found a skilled cannery man to take charge of the job, but he must have a crew to help him, and Charlie had promised men from the sawmill.

'I hope you told them we'd pay them extra wages to go down there,' Rod said to the sawmill owner. 'It's well worth it to us.'

'Extra!' Charlie's voice rose to a thin screech. 'Pay them what I pay them! They're already fighting to be the ones to go. When do you need them?'

'In a few days, as soon as we've taken down the webbing. Jeff and Mom are coming from Hidden Harbour this afternoon, and tomorrow Jeff and Spence and I will take the first load.'

The next morning they loaded the scow with half the webbing, all the big rolls they could pile on. With the *Taku* and Rod's motor boat towing, they ran it down the strait and unloaded it on a flat bench above high tide.

It was the first time Jeff had seen the river to which he'd pledged so much. Rod had been a bit fearful he might find it disappointing. This was so different a battle than he'd ever fought before. Their weapons lay spread out before them, two enormous floating traps and a pile of wire webbing on the shore. Jeff's eyes gleamed as he surveyed them.

'Daniels said we couldn't build 'em!' He chuckled. 'Just like he says this river won't have a pink run. He don't know Alaska. It's too big a country for a man like him to take its measure. Or of the folks who growed up in it.' He grinned at Rod and started toward their boats. 'Let's get back. Sooner we get that last jag of web here, the sooner we'll be set.'

They started late the next night with the second half of webbing, rolls piled high on the scow. The weather looked good, the tide was right. But later on the strait a strong south-east wind blew against the ebb. Spray was breaking over the scow. Rod was worried as the two boats chugged on abreast, but the big ebb was helping and the load of webbing was riding steady. After a couple of hours he was sure they would make it. So was Jeff, as he called to Rod from the wheelhouse of the *Taku*. It was long past midnight, when they were almost at Tallac Bay, that a sudden gust came off the mountainside. Spence, thinking of the reefs, opened his throttle wide. His line tightened, then snapped. Rod felt the shock on his own line as it took the whole load of the scow. It stopped the motor boat, dragged it back despite full power.

The *Taku* had shot ahead, but now Spence brought it back, his searchlight on. As he manoeuvred so that Jeff could cast a new line to the scow, Rod felt another and harder shock, and looking back in the searchlight's beam he saw the scow had struck a sloping reef. Slowly it tipped up. A wave slapped it higher. Rolls of webbing broke from their lashings and catapulted into the sea. In seconds the scow was nearly empty. Then, lightened of its load and boosted by a wave, it responded to the line from Rod's boat and slipped free.

Rod had a sick feeling. All he could think of was that they had lost the webbing for the second trap. The *Taku* came up, Jeff made a line fast, they towed the scow into the bay and lifted the remaining five rolls of webbing to the beach.

'You know what this did!' Rod said. 'Five hundred dollars' worth of wire webbing gone just a month before the traps have got to be ready.'

His tone was savage. After all these months of work one broken line had brought disaster. If Spence or Jeff felt they'd had enough he couldn't blame them. But now they'd have to go on, no matter how they felt. With all that work and money put in the frame, steel cable, anchors, and all the gear for the second trap, they couldn't lose it for just five hundred dollars.

'I suppose when the law says a working trap, it means one with wire webbing in it,' Jeff said. 'Well, we ain't going to lose the right to run that river like we ought to for just five hundred dollars. Gives us quite a piece to go on the trail yet. But that happens sometimes. How about you, Spence?'

'We'll get there somehow,' Spence said. 'When I come back from Shallow Creek tonight, we'll talk about it.'

Spence had planned to make a delivery on the strait while Jeff and Rod towed the empty scow back to Rampart. Spence helped them out of the bay, then cast off, and the *Taku* started south. Rod watched as it disappeared down the channel and thought of the months and months Spence had driven himself to do the work of two men. Now he intended to mortgage the *Taku*. Rod knew this was what he must have meant. It was their only answer, but could he let Spence do this? Yet otherwise, Spence would lose all he had invested in the second trap. And without it there was no hope of safeguarding the river, keeping it stocked and fertile for the years ahead. Then Rod asked himself if he was sure enough that the pinks would always return. Could he possibly be mistaken?

These questions were gnawing at him on the run back to Rampart, questions he couldn't share with Jeff. After a long silence his father spoke.

'Funny thing, Rod, how you and me never went hunting together like Spence and I used to. Getting your bear, when he's coming for you—you get to know the fellow who's standing alongside you awful well. We never done that together, Rod, and when you was a kid, I felt sort of bad about it. But then I didn't know your bears were different like. . . .' He paused a moment. 'Well—like this river and building up the salmon is your sort of bear. And you'll get him. I ain't afeared of that, son.'

At the moment Jeff's speech gave Rod a tremendous lift, but back at Rampart Bay the questions crowded in again. He looked across at the cannery and wondered if Daniels could be right about one or two runs on a river meaning nothing. He didn't think so, but the idea of Spence mortgaging the *Taku* had upset him. Yet they couldn't lose all they'd spent on the two traps for just this one last setback.

Rod left the store and went down to the freight shed. He wanted to be alone. Only the day before he had written so confidently to Judy that the traps would be ready and waiting for the harvest when she arrived. A harvest that would bring security and comfort to the Bairds in the years ahead. That had been part of his dream.

He heard the sound of rowlocks and looked out as Charlie Reynolds brought his skiff alongside the float. Rod went to meet him.

'As you ought to know by this time, I'm a tight old codger,' Charlie said. 'Never lent a cent except I knew it was a sure thing. But that don't mean you and Jeff and Spence have got to put up security. You're Bairds, ain't you? That's enough for me, and you don't have to tell me you got nothing left. How much do you need to get web for that second trap?'

'About five hundred. And I'll give you a mortgage on the store.'

Charlie waved this idea aside. 'Wouldn't know what to do with it. Sawmill's grief enough.' He pulled out a roll of bills and handed them to Rod. 'Give you a cheque if you'd rather, but I thought you could send a money order on the *Resolute* tomorrow. Might save a few days and time's getting short. Pay me when you're good and ready.'

He shoved off before Rod had recovered enough to speak. In one moment Rod had gone from despair to new hope, and he was still dazed when he rushed to the store to tell Jeff and Mary. His mother wasn't at all amazed.

'Charlie knew you needed that webbing in a hurry, and he wouldn't waste a minute getting down here. Isn't it wonderful how all Rampart feels about that river and the Bairds!'

So the two traps were in place, the webbing was hung, the leads stretched to shore, and everything readied for the coming of the salmon. The Bairds were broke. They had less than fifty dollars among the lot and owed Charlie Reynolds five hundred. But for once neither Jeff nor Spence spoke of debt with foreboding.

All they talked of was the June run of pinks at Tallac River.

15

As Judy waited for the *Queen*'s gangplank to be lowered, she was thinking of her first arrival, only a year before. The scene was exactly as it had been then—the crowd on the wharf to meet the ship, the row of Indian women sitting along the freight shed with their wares set out before them, and the tourists gathered on the deck around her, eager not to miss a moment of their day of sight-seeing. But for her it was different.

This was a homecoming.

She hurried down the gangplank into the arms of her father. He kissed her, than held her off for a good look. 'We've missed you, Judy! It's good to have you back.'

'And so wonderful to be here,' she said. She shook hands with Alec, then impulsively threw her arms around him, which embarrassed him a bit but pleased him enormously. 'It's wonderful to see you both,' she repeated. 'And I hope we're leaving for Shaman Cove right away.'

Alec was already collecting luggage. As they walked down the long wharf and turned to the pier where the small craft were moored, Judy drank in the familiar sounds and smells of the water front. The motor boats, tied so sociably bow to stern, brought a sense of the real Alaska. Alec put the bags down beside a strange boat.

'But what's happened to the *Working Stiff*?' she demanded. 'You didn't wreck her!'

'Sound as ever. We needed this one'—Alec nodded at the black-hulled fifty-footer—'to handle heavy machinery. Carl, here, is the skipper. Got promoted from the engine crew.'

Carl grinned and carried the bags aboard while Alec gave Judy a hand to help her up.

'Ain't got no accommodation ladder,' he explained. 'Boat ain't any fancier than her name, *Betsy*. Just a good solid chunk of work boat.' The *Betsy* was all of that, Judy thought, as she felt the afterdeck shiver beneath her feet when the heavy motor started and they pulled out into the stream. 'You're still skipper of the *Working Stiff*,' he added, 'if that's what's bothering you.'

It had been, but she didn't know she'd shown it. Now she looked back at the town, nestled beneath a mountain and gleaming in the bright sunshine, and thought what a wonderful day for a homecoming.

'Want to go below?' her father asked.

'Not yet. I don't want to miss a moment of this.' Her wave included the sparkling channel and the mainland mountains rearing their white-crowned heads. 'Do you mind?' she added, looking somewhat dubiously at the broad deck piled with heavy freight.

'Not a bit,' he said and found a box big enough for them to sit on. 'Like it better out here myself.'

Alec rechecked the lashings of the freight. 'Don't want this ore cart to rare around when we hit the strait,' he said, and then smiled at Judy. 'Did the Boss tell you we've driven the tunnel a hundred and fifty feet?' He went forward to the wheelhouse.

Judy's eyes were glowing as she turned to her father. 'Does that mean it's going to be a real mine? And you're staying in Alaska?'

'Looks like it.' There was a note of quiet satisfaction in his voice. 'We've decided to get out ore. I'm in charge of production, and at a considerable boost in salary, I might add. But it was gratifying to have the director accept my findings and suggestions without question.' And then, almost as an afterthought, he said, 'Not that I mean this was of any great importance to anyone except myself.'

She smiled. It was terribly important, and to them both. Now surely he could stop brooding about the Lady Luck. She was almost certain that he had. The old buoyancy, which she'd remembered in him and had missed last summer, was all back as he told of the new plans for the mine. The president of the company and his wife would spend several weeks at Shaman Cove, and they'd need a real guest house. Judy thought she'd like to help Alec build one. 'And

I'll have to be in Juneau quite a bit this summer, may go to California, so we'll have town busts together,' he said. He had made a business trip to Seattle, seen Mr Daniels, and met the Richards. Mrs Richards had said Chris Daniels was coming to Rampart Bay on the *Chasima* in August and suggested that Judy join them for a short cruise.

'So you see this summer won't be so lonely for you, Judy,' he finished.

'But I wasn't lonely last year,' she said.

She hadn't meant to seem quite so on the defensive, but it bothered her to have him dismiss last summer so casually. He knew it hadn't been lonely. It was a summer she would remember always, and she'd been hoping he would tell her something about the Bairds, but instead he asked about her trip in the Orient.

'I knew you must be having a wonderful time,' he added. 'I was sure of it from your letters.'

'I did! It would take weeks to tell you all we did and what we saw. Aunt Nina sends her love and said to tell you if she hadn't invited June house guests, she would have come on to Alaska with me.'

'I thought she would enjoy a few weeks up here when I asked her.'

'And she would! She was fascinated by the things I told her about the country and the people. She'd never realized it was all so—so excitingly different. In the East, people don't seem to know anything about Alaska. She hadn't much idea about it even from my letters.'

Her father smiled. 'After all, you could tell her only about Shaman Cove and Rampart Bay. That's hardly—'

'And the Inside Passage,' she said quickly. 'I've travelled that three times now. Besides, you know a country better when you've actually lived in it and really know the people. It's all the difference between belonging and—' She hesitated. 'I don't feel like an outsider any more—the way I did when I first came up here.'

It was all so different from the year before. Shaman Cove established as a mine, her father living in Alaska, and the plans he'd made for their summer showed so plainly he wanted her to stay. Yet, so far, he hadn't spoken about the Bairds. Sooner or later, he or Alec must surely do so.

It was afternoon before she asked about them, when she couldn't wait any longer.

Her father said he hadn't seen them lately. 'With two boats and a regular skipper, we don't need the *Taku* freight service. But Daniels told me they had finally built their traps.'

The 'finally' sounded ominous. 'I know,' she said. 'Rod wrote me Jeff built them in Rampart Bay.'

'Oh!' He looked at her in some surprise. 'You heard from him?'

'Yes. And he told me how the trollers towed them to Tallac River. Just imagine thirty boats with their running lights all on and pulling together to help out a neighbour. Like an old-time barn-raising, Alaska-style.'

'And tragic too, don't you think, Judy?'

She stiffened. 'Because Rod had loyal friends?'

'No. Because the Bairds had no funds to hire a tug. Jeff had wasted a winter's work, Spence had used his savings, and still they went on! After they lost that scow of wire webbing, Daniels doesn't know where they got the money to buy more, but they did somehow. Probably mortgaged the *Taku*, unless they'd already done so. It's—it's indefensible, Judy, what Rod has let his family in for. Broke. And in debt for years perhaps.'

She felt a little sick. After all these months, she'd come back to the same old trouble, the same old question. And she'd been so sure she'd no longer have to defend Rod, only think of him as a person.

'Then you still believe the salmon won't come?' she said.

'Naturally I accept the opinion of experienced salmon men.' He glanced at her briefly, then looked away, as he added, 'And I've been hoping you would, Judy, after a winter to think it over and see things in their proper focus.'

'That was the idea of my going, wasn't it?' she asked in a strained voice.

'Partly, perhaps,' he said. 'But not entirely, by any means. I'm sure we talked about this before you went, Judy.'

She nodded.

She didn't want to talk about it now, didn't even feel the need to defend Rod as her father went on quoting Mr Daniels. It was the same old story of his concern about the Bairds and of the years he had spent in the salmon industry. Nothing except actually seeing the Tallac pinks fighting their way upriver would convince her father how autocratic the canner's opinions were.

'I'm only asking you to be reasonable about this, Judy,' he ended.

'But what's the use of all this now, Dad! It's done. The traps are built, aren't they? Maybe the Bairds are broke! And in debt too! I don't know. But it's only two weeks before the run. Can't we just wait—like—like they are doing and not tear—everything apart?' She was close to tears. 'This was my homecoming.'

'And I ought not to have brought this up, Judy!' he exclaimed contritely. 'I'd intended not to.' He put his arm around her. 'I never meant to spoil this day, but I've been worried for you, Judy. It wasn't your fault you became so worked up about Tallac River last summer. In this place you had nothing else to think about! I'm to blame for ever bringing you up here. I know this. I've always known it. And we will wait before we talk about it. We won't speak of this again until—' and he paused—'until there's no question about the outcome.'

'Thanks, Dad.' She wiped her eyes. 'It's—it's only I can't bear to hear you talk like Daniels!'

For the rest of the day, and in those following, they scrupulously avoided any mention of the river. And this only made them more aware of the chasm that lay between them.

Sang was overjoyed to have a zealous shopper again. With the increased crew, a cook's needs were imperative, and Carl always forgot important items. Judy promised to supply them and went to Rampart the second day after her arrival.

The store's float looked deserted with Rod's motor boat gone and no *Taku*. Henry Dane came out of the freight shed to take the lines.

'Where's everybody?' she asked.

'Rod and Jeff are at the traps. Spence won't be in till late tonight. He's sure pushing gas through the *Taku* these days. And Mrs Baird is running the store.'

Judy hurried up the path, opened the door, and called, 'Hello!' Mary Baird came out of the office.

'Judy!' she cried, and rushed across the store with open arms. 'It's good to see you! When did you get back?'

'Two days ago. It's wonderful to be here. I was coming this afternoon even if Sang hadn't needed anything. Henry says you're running the store!'

Mary laughed. 'Henry's being generous. He's the one who's taking care of everything. He really is,' she insisted when Judy smiled. 'Nothing is too much trouble for him. And the trollers! Half the time they put up their own orders and even write the sales slips.'

'Doesn't Rod have to be here at all?'

'He comes every Saturday evening, takes stock and writes wholesale orders on Sunday. So you see, I'm just a fraud as a storekeeper.'

'But you like it!' Judy laughed. 'I can see that.'

'I do.' Mary's eyes were a bit misty. 'I never knew we had so many neighbours. All the trollers on the strait. The men at the sawmill. Even the crew on the *Resolute*. All so anxious to do something.' Then suddenly she became very brisk. 'But we can talk while we put up your order.'

'It's a long list,' Judy said.

They piled groceries on the counter as they chatted. There was so much to catch up on. Judy told about her winter in the Orient, and Mary gave her the news of Rampart Bay.

'Will you stay in the store all summer?' Judy asked.

'Only while Jeff is helping Rod watch the traps. Rod has found a man to do it later. But right now—'

'Of course!' Judy broke in quickly, not wanting Mary to have to explain they had no money for extra wages. 'Jeff would want to be there when the salmon come. It won't be long now.'

Mary nodded 'The middle of June. It's always been an early run. The Indians used to count on it.'

Judy looked at the calendar on the wall. 'Why, the fifteenth is only six days away!'

She found this a bit frightening, and for a time they worked in silence, each busy with her own thoughts. Then Mary smiled.

'I don't think even Vicky's coming with Phil and the baby could drag Jeff away from Tallac right now. I told her so when she was so sorry they couldn't be here until August.'

'Then she knows about the river?'

'She was the only one who knew from the beginning. That's why she'd planned to come this June, but Phil had a big order for illustrations in a magazine that's never used his work before. And he'd always hoped they would.'

'How marvellous! She must have been so proud to write and tell you that.' Then Judy added a little wistfully, 'And to know how happy it would make you.'

'Yes.' Mary's face glowed with deep content. 'Vicky said that if any more wonderful things happened to her this year, she didn't think she could bear it. Tallac River. Our building the traps when sometimes it looked as though we couldn't. Philip's big chance falling in his lap so suddenly. And then bringing young Jeff home for a visit. It is all sort of wonderful. But she and Phil deserve it. You'll like them both, Judy.'

'I do already. How long will they stay?'

'Until October. Phil wants to wait until the Indians are home from fishing and then do some sketching in the Tlingit village.' She added a few cans to the collection on the counter. 'That finishes the list. Henry will put it in your boat.'

'You know I haven't seen the traps yet,' Judy said.

'Neither have I, not since they were towed from Rampart. Rod has been too busy to take me.'

'But I can! Why don't you come home with me today, and tomorrow morning we'll go to Tallac Bay and surprise them. If we get an early start, I could bring you back that night.'

'But you wouldn't have to,' Mary said. 'Rod can bring me when he comes on Saturday.'

David Randolph came down to the float to greet them.

'Mrs Baird!' he exclaimed. 'This is wonderful! It's been so long since I've seen you, and I've never had an opportunity to thank you for Judy's delightful week-end in Hidden Harbour. And how is Jeff?'

'Fine, Rod tells me. I haven't seen him for weeks and weeks, and now Judy will take me over there tomorrow. I'm so excited about our going.'

'I can imagine.' He smiled and picked up her bag. 'It looks as though you girls will have a good day to cross the strait.' At the door of the house he handed the bag to Judy. 'I'll tell Sang we have a guest. There's no hurry. We'll wait until the crew has eaten.'

When they went to supper, it was evident he'd urged Sang to make a special effort. The table was impressive with a fresh cloth, flowers in the centre, and a first course of crab cocktail at each plate.

'This is a real party!' Mary exclaimed in pleasure.

'I'd thought I had a bottle of wine around here somewhere, but it appears I haven't,' David Randolph said. 'Next time, we'll celebrate it properly. What's the news in Rampart? Did Daniels get his new machinery installed?'

'Oh, yes. The cannery was ready a week ago, and all the Indians are settled on the point waiting to go to work.'

Judy had a sense of quick relief. They couldn't have gone on for hours avoiding the subject of salmon with everyone in the country waiting for them. But Mary Baird had answered without the slightest evidence of strain. She hadn't sounded at all like a person who was possibly facing ruin.

She continued on this note all evening. A question from David Randolph about their coming to Alaska started her on an absorbing story of their early years, and he became so fascinated he wouldn't let her stop even after she protested they surely must have heard enough. She told homely little details of the slim days in the beginning when she'd used flour sacks to make the children's clothing and contrived so many things they couldn't afford to buy. Nor did she leave out the really tough times, the setbacks, when Jeff had refused to admit defeat, and her own challenges as a mother of a growing family. She'd had only a country school certificate and had had to study in the evenings when her children were ready to tackle high-school subjects. 'And sometimes we studied them together,' she laughed. But she spoke of her and Jeff's problems almost casually, only remembering their joy when they had met them.

It was, Judy thought, like sharing an exciting adventure tale. Her father was as enthralled as she was. In a way the recital had completed, and made more real and more moving, Jeff's long search for a country.

'I'm so glad we had those years,' Mary said. 'I know some people haven't understood and perhaps they've felt it wasn't right. Sometimes even I have wondered. But now—' She hesitated for a moment. 'Now I'm sure that sharing those years must have made it easier for Vicky when she too had to go to a strange, new country.'

For a moment David Randolph seemed puzzled, then exclaimed, 'I see what you mean! New York and Greenwich Village must have been the same challenge in pioneering to a girl who'd only known Hidden Harbour! She needed all the courage and self-reliance those years had taught her. Needed to have had a mother like you,' he added. 'You've told all this as though it were ordinary, but you've failed to hide from me the wonderful spirit without which none of this could ever have happened.'

Mary's soft laugh was disbelieving.

'I only did what any woman would do. And they were happy years.' She arose. 'I've kept you up and done all the talking, but I've had a lovely time. Will I see you in the morning to say good-bye?'

'You're coming back with Judy tomorrow evening, surely!' he protested.

'No. Rod will take me home the next day when they close the traps.'

'Close?' he asked.

'Lift the net,' she explained. 'Traps have to be closed from Saturday evening until Monday morning.'

'You mean if those fish should come during a weekend,

you couldn't catch them?' Judy demanded in a tone of horror.

'Rod wouldn't. The law is right. Some fish must get up-river to seed the stream. There's nothing more important than the seed for another harvest. I was a farmer's daughter and I know.'

'But I thought you people came from the Kentucky mountains!' David Randolph said.

'Jeff did. The Bairds had lived there for generations. I was a Western girl.'

'Then how did Jeff ever have the good fortune to find you?' he asked. 'I've been wanting to ask all evening.'

Mary blushed. 'He was just riding through the town where I taught school, on his way to the next range. And I don't think he would have stopped if he hadn't wanted a drink of water and seen the schoolhouse pump.' She paused, and then she added, 'And I've never been sorry that he did.'

16

As Judy approached Tallac Bay next morning, she kept the *Working Stiff* well offshore until she got her bearings, to avoid the dangerous reefs stretching from either point of the entrance. Then she turned in sharply. Ahead, she could see the black lines of the two traps with an absurdly little shack atop of each.

'They've even built their watchmen's houses!' Mary Baird cried in excitement. 'And look! They've seen us! Blow your whistle, Judy!'

Judy sounded the signal of three staccato blasts, and Rod waved a jubilant greeting from the first trap. She swung towards it and in a moment was alongside. He pulled the boat close to the big trap timber and reached out to grab her hands.

'I was hoping you would come, Judy,' he said, and his eyes were glowing as he looked at her almost hungrily. 'And Mom too! Both of you together! How'd it happen?'

'It was Judy's idea,' his mother said. 'We wanted to surprise you boys, and it appears we did. Here comes Jeff from the other trap!'

'I'll shove the boat along to the platform so you can get out,' Rod said. 'Had a little rain this morning, and the timbers are still slippery.'

They were disembarked on the platform when Jeff came running along a timber so fast the sharp steel caulks in his shoes tore off splinters. He enveloped Mary in a bear hug, and then shook hands with Judy.

'Did you think of this, Judy?' She nodded. 'Best idea you ever had. Ain't it, Rod? It's a good thing we ain't broke up our camp ashore. These shacks'—and he scowled at the small structure raised three feet above the trap—'now we got a bed and stove in 'em, they ain't big enough for one fellow to turn around in, let alone the four of us. Tell you what! Let's leave your boat here and all go ashore in my skiff.'

'But can't I see the traps?' Judy asked.

'I've been waiting for a month to show them to you,' Rod said. 'You people go ahead. We'll come in later.'

Jeff nodded and turned to Mary. 'Rod dug a pail of clams this morning. Got all the makings of a chowder, and now we got the finest chowder-maker in the country with us. How about it?'

'Are they shucked?' Mary asked.

'No, but I'd be proud to do it for you.'

'Why, Jeff!' Mary laughed happily. 'And I'm going to let you do it while I sit and watch.'

'Fair enough,' he agreed. 'I tell you, Judy! Until you've tasted one of Mary's chowders, with plenty of salt pork and onions and potatoes, you don't know what chowder's like.'

Judy watched them as Jeff pulled away, with Mary in the stern. 'Aren't they sweet together? And wasn't he pleased to see her? They'd really rather be alone while we look at the traps.'

'Which wasn't why I— Oh, Judy! Sometimes I thought you were never coming back!'

'But I'd promised I would come.'

She flushed and looked away. Her awareness of him was terribly disturbing. Sometimes the past winter she had wondered if missing him so acutely, thinking of him so often, had been part of the confusion of last summer and her feeling of the need to defend him. Now that she was with him, she suddenly felt strange and very shy. Then she saw that he was staring at her in a puzzled fashion.

'It's wonderful to be back,' she went on a little raggedly. 'Only I've hardly caught my breath yet.' Her eyes pleaded that he understand. 'But I couldn't wait to see the traps. Aren't you going to show one to me?'

'Of course.' His voice was strained, and then he smiled. 'It's all right, Judy,' he said. 'It was only—well I couldn't make it seem real you were really back until I saw you—' He untied the rowing boat, helped her in, and shipped the oars. 'If we start at the shore end of the trap, you'll understand it better. Now you pretend you're a Tallac pink and

168

you've come down the strait on your way to your home river.'

She giggled, feeling suddenly relaxed and joyous. Only Rod would make a game of this. 'But how can I be sure a purse seiner won't catch me at the entrance? Won't they be waiting for me?'

'They can't. That's the beauty of this river. With those reefs off both points, a purse seiner couldn't set a net.'

'So Mr Daniels and his seine boats haven't caught me,' she said with considerable satisfaction.

'No. And you've come around the point and along the shore of the bay and run into this wall of wire web.'

He had rowed close to the shore. Far down, Judy could see the webbing disappearing into the water's darkness. It was exactly like a wall, running at right angles from the shore and hanging from a cable attached to cedar floats.

'So naturally I turn and swim along it, looking for a way out,' she said.

'But where do you get to?' Rod rowed along the lead until they came to timbers set in a V-shape and heavily braced. 'Into the hearts. Web hangs from these logs and keeps you swimming to the point of the V. If you try to go down, you run into the web apron, which leads you up into the next heart. Always higher. And the point of the V leads to a narrow tunnel. It looks like a way out. And you're a pink, wanting to get to home stream. So you try it. Wait.' He rowed closer. 'See it down there. It's a bag of cotton web. Of course you suppose it's the way to escape. But it narrows. You go through and you're in the pot, that big square in the middle of the trap. Thirty by thirty feet and twenty-four feet deep.'

'But I wouldn't keep going through narrow places trying to get up river!' she protested.

'Sure you would! You're a salmon and you'd do more than that to reach home stream. You'd even leap up falls to get to spawning grounds. You're driven by a homing instinct. So when you swim into the pot of the trap, you'll still go on trying to find a way out. I'll show you.'

He rowed around to the hundred-foot face of the trap,

stepped out on a log, and made the boat fast. 'I'll hold you,' he said, reaching his hands to her. 'Walk behind me. I can't slip with these corks.'

They walked to the centre of the face. 'That's where you came through from the hearts,' he said, pointing into the clear water. 'Now you're in the pot, all surrounded by wire web, but still trying to get to your river. Only way out is through two more tunnels. See them, one on either side, nice big openings, and you don't know they narrow at the other end. So you swim through, into one of the spillers. There's no way out from there. You swim around and around and never see the narrow opening you came through.'

'And I'm caught! In a Baird trap!'

Rod started. His mouth opened, but he did not speak for a moment. Then he said quietly, 'I hope so, Judy.'

She flushed, started to turn on the wet log, slipped, and gripped his hand more tightly.

'I almost was,' she laughed. 'And then I'd have to swim around and around. But, Rod'—and she was suddenly serious—'I never dreamed a trap was so—so complicated. From a boat they looked so simple, just a frame of timbers floating on the sea. But all that webbing and tunnels and so deep in the water! No wonder they cost so much. I never could quite believe it, even when Mr Daniels told us.'

She felt him look at her quickly, saw him turn and stare into the empty water of the spiller. After a moment he spoke.

'Our traps didn't, in a way,' he said. 'If a canner had built this trap, it would have cost him five thousand dollars. We beat that by a lot, Jeff having the timber, doing the work ourselves, getting a break on secondhand cable and anchors, and having friends step in and help us out when we thought we were licked. A lot of things have gone into these traps, Judy. Some, maybe, you don't know about.' She nodded. She couldn't have spoken. She wondered if it wasn't this Rod, this thoughtful Rod, of all the many sides he seemed to have, who stirred her most. And then suddenly his voice quickened. 'But the luckiest break of all was this sheltered bay, and a river everybody said had been fished out. Gave us a chance to prove you can bring back a run of pinks.'

'And that was why you had to do it!'

'Partly. Naturally, we thought about what the traps would catch. Say we took only three hundred thousand fish this year and let all the others go upriver to spawn. That's a low catch for two traps. A canner wouldn't be satisfied. But at six cents a fish, which is what Daniels is paying this year, look what it would mean to the Bairds. Eighteen thousand dollars! And a bigger catch the next year! Jeff and Mom could take it easier, Spence could get a real freight boat and a man to help him. And Vicky—why, she never had even a wedding present or the right clothes to go to New York in. And old Sha-goon-e-ish!' He laughed. 'He and Jennie could have all the tobacco and molasses and grub they'll need the rest of their lives!'

'And you, Rod?' she asked.

He flushed. 'The way I've been sounding off you'd think the traps were already filled with fish.'

'But they will come, Rod!' she cried almost fiercely. 'I— I know they will!'

It seemed that saying so would make it all come true.

'Still pulling for me, aren't you, Judy,' and his handclasp tightened. 'What do you say we go upriver and have a look at the riffles? Maybe a few have come. I haven't been up this morning.'

'Shouldn't we go ashore and help with—'

'Jeff wouldn't let us even stir Mom's chowder.' He started for his rowing boat.

They rowed to the head of the bay. The trail along the beach and up the river was worn now. Judy thought how often Rod must have walked over it, going upstream, looking, waiting, hoping.

They sat on a big boulder beside the riffles where Sha-goon-e-ish had counted salmon.

'Not even a few first-comers,' Rod said, 'and this was always the earliest river around here.'

'But it's still five days until the fifteenth. And the cannery had no fish yesterday when I was in Rampart.'

He nodded and seemed to find comfort in this fact. For a

few moments they sat in silence. Judy was thinking how wonderful it was to be with Rod again, and beside a river, when he suddenly began to talk.

'In the beginning I wouldn't have expected Daniels to believe that clearing out a stream could bring back a run of pinks. Plenty of times those first two years I didn't dare believe it myself, Judy. But you'd think he'd believe it now after I told him about the run last summer. And be glad to believe it, because it's the canners who have got to save the salmon and save their own necks at the same time. The government isn't doing much. They can't, with the few patrol boats and men they have. But if the fellows in the fishery bureau would get the canners pulling with them, knowing everybody's got to work together, they could do a lot.

'Then the canners would see how it made sense to keep track of runs and spawners, even close a river if it was being overfished and let the stock build up again. And you can't tell me the canners wouldn't see it, if the fishery bureau went at it right. The canners have got to see it, if they expect to go on packing salmon like in the old days.

'Alaska is a rich country, Judy,' he said earnestly, and then he smiled. 'Funny thing, but when I was a kid, I used to think a lot about how rich this country is, and every time I saw Richards' yacht at the cannery, I'd tell myself some day I'd have a bigger yacht than he had. He started with only a little sawmill, smaller even than Charlie Reynolds'. But now—Well, that big yacht doesn't worry me a bit. Perhaps I'm too much like Jeff and the way he feels about the kind of country he wants to live in. Anyway, I've been thinking a lot about salmon streams and what could be done about them.' He was silent for a moment. 'I just thought I ought to tell you, Judy, so you'd know about me.'

'I always knew. I—I've known ever since that afternoon you first told me about the river.'

'You have! And then, maybe some day, if I'm right about this river, I can tell you how—'

'You don't have to be right about the river!' she said in a choked voice. 'That—that doesn't matter. Not any more.'

'You mean—' His face lighted with wonder and a sudden joy. 'I never thought this—this—' And then she was in his arms. 'Oh, Judy, Judy,' he said. 'I loved you from the first day I saw you.'

She knew this wasn't quite true, but it was wonderful of him to think so.

They sat by the river for a long time. They didn't make plans. They couldn't, but they could tell each other how empty the winter had been and how they'd longed to see each other and all the things they'd thought and never said before.

It was Judy who first remembered Mary's chowder. She leaped to her feet. 'It must have been ready for hours!' she cried. 'What will they imagine has happened to us?'

'Can I tell them you're my girl, Judy?' Rod asked.

She hesitated, thinking of her father. It would be so much easier to tell him after the salmon had come to Rod's river.

'Let's not tell anyone for a little while,' she said. 'You and I know it, and that's all that counts.'

'Sure.' Rod grinned. 'And Mom and Jeff will know it anyway. Couldn't help but know when they see me looking at you.'

17

JUDY WOKE early. The fifteenth of June had come at last. For four days she hadn't allowed herself to look at the calendar. The old adage that a watched kettle never boils might not be true, but not watching it made the time go faster. And now Mary Baird must certainly have news about the river. At breakfast she announced she was going to Rampart Bay.

Alec was dubious. 'By afternoon the strait will be tough.'

Her father looked up alertly. 'And whatever Sang needs, it can't be that important.'

'But I'd promised to lend some books to Mrs Baird.' It was the only errand she could think of at the moment. For once Sang had failed her. 'With nothing much to do at the store, she really needs them. I can be back by noon.'

'How about it, Alec?' her father asked.

'Sure,' Alec said. 'If she gets an early start.'

Mary Baird was opening the store when she arrived.

'Why, Judy!' Mary exclaimed in surprise. 'You make me feel so lazy! Henry isn't even up yet. We had so many trollers in last night. But you shouldn't have come all this way to bring me books.' She read the titles, and her eyes glowed when she saw an anthology of modern poetry.

'Aunt Nina gave it to me, and I thought you'd like it,' Judy explained.

'I'll read myself to sleep tonight.'

'Has the pink run started?' Judy asked.

'Not at Tallac. The cannery has been running for two days, so it can't be long now.' Mary's tone was confident. 'Spence was here last night. He'd been in to see Rod and Jeff.'

'Hadn't any salmon come at all? Not even a few?'

'Not yet. But nobody can guess just how or when they'll come. The cannery was ready and waiting for a week with everyone, even the Indians at the point, on tenterhooks.

Then all of a sudden, the cannery had steam up and every Tlingit was working, except the old grandmothers. And they are busy taking care of the children. Now everyone is happy.'

Judy looked across the bay at the Indian encampment, where little columns of smoke were rising from scores of cooking fires. The small community bore a look of contentment. Somehow it was reassuring.

'And the pinks will come just as suddenly at Tallac,' Mary went on after a moment. Her hand rested lightly on Judy's shoulder, and her eyes were warm with understanding. 'Any day now.'

'I know,' Judy said. 'I wasn't really worried. I'd just hoped—' Her words trailed off. Of course Mrs Baird knew why she'd come rushing up to Rampart Bay so early in the morning.

'If it isn't blowing too hard to cross the strait, I'm going to Tallac tomorrow,' Judy said.

Mary's eyes brightened. 'I wish you would! And tell Rod that Henry and I have taken care of the wholesale orders so he won't have to leave Tallac this weekend.' Judy nodded. Then Mary was counting the days just as she was and believing with all her heart because it was all they could do now. 'Haven't you time for a cup of coffee?' Mary asked. 'I've just made a fresh pot.'

They drank it sitting on the high stools at the trollers' counter. Mary showed young Jeff's latest pictures and talked of Vicky's coming visit. Neither spoke of the river. Later, on her way home, Judy decided not to go to Rampart Bay again until the Tallac run had come. Waiting was hard enough for Mary without having to talk about it.

Next morning Sang packed a lunch for three, and Judy departed. It was almost noon when she turned into Tallac Bay. Rod and Jeff waved from the first trap, and she ran alongside the platform at the foot of the watchman's shack.

'I knew you'd come today!' Rod said as he made her boat fast. He reached out and lifted her to the platform. 'Just as wonderful as ever,' he whispered as Jeff came along the log.

'Been hoping you'd come over,' Jeff said, then saw her staring at the long pole in his hand. 'Rod and I have been cleaning web.'

'I thought you only watched it,' Judy laughed.

'Sounds that way, don't it?' Jeff chuckled. 'But we don't want the pinks to get a notion this might be a trap, when they do come.' He reached down, hauled out a long string of seaweed, tossed it overside, then leaned the pole against the shack. 'Guess that cleans yours up, lad, and long's I got my skiff, I'm goin' ashore and cut a little jag o' wood. See you afore you go, Judy.'

'But I brought a picnic lunch for all of us. Sang made a special cake.'

'So?' Jeff's eyes gleamed. 'I'll build a fire ashore, and we'll make a pot of coffee.'

She watched Jeff row away. He hadn't sounded like a man who was disheartened. Nor did he look it. 'I hope he didn't think he had to run away,' she said.

'Not a bit,' Rod assured her. 'He feels cooped up on these traps, but he doesn't grouch about it. Take a look at the shack and you'll understand how he feels about them. Then we'll sit aboard your boat.'

She peered through the open door. A bunk, a stove, and a box that served as table filled the space completely.

'I don't see how you can stand it!' she said. 'Will you have to live in this all summer?'

'As long as the run lasts. We'll hire another watchman to take Jeff's place, but I'll have to be here, I want to make sure enough spawners get upriver.'

He seemed so confident they would come. And as they sat in the cabin of the *Working Stiff* and talked about it, she wondered why she'd been so worried because the fifteenth had come and gone. She told him of her early morning trip to Rampart Bay and that the cannery was operating. None of this was news to Rod.

'Spence stopped in again last night,' he said. 'The cannery isn't going full blast. Seiners have made some good hauls, but we don't know how the traps are doing. Spence is going to find out.'

'Your mother says the Tallac pinks will come all of a sudden.'

'They didn't last year, or the year before that.' His face was serious. 'Both years had an early dribble, but so far there hasn't been a single fish in either trap or any in the riffles I was upriver this morning.'

'Haven't they ever been late before?'

'Not in the last two years. Before that, all I know is what Sha-goon-e-ish told me, and no Indian is very clear on time. All we can do is wait.' He smiled at her. 'Will you come over often? It helps a lot, Judy.'

'Every day I can,' she said.

He drew her closer. 'But don't you come unless Alec says it's all right. I don't want you on that strait when it's nasty.'

She laughed. This was a new Rod, a possessive Rod, but she found she liked it. 'There's no chance I ever would be, Alec wouldn't let me. And aren't you afraid Jeff is getting very hungry? He's built a fire, and I think I smell coffee.'

She stayed until mid-afternoon and went over again the next day. Rod was waiting for her.

'I didn't want to miss this good day because there will be some when I can't come,' she explained.

'That's how I was hoping you would think,' Rod said. 'Mind staying at the trap? Jeff's gone upriver, and someone ought to be on one of them at least.'

She glanced at him quickly. Then he was more worried than he admitted. 'Let's sit on those steps and eat our sandwiches in the sun,' she said, handing him the picnic basket. 'I don't know what Sang gave us this time, but I think he sent a pie.'

'Aren't you ever going to try my cooking? I'm all settled so I can fix a meal of sorts. When the trap is fishing, I won't get ashore much.'

'Does it bother Jeff—the salmon—not—not coming yet?' she asked, then added, 'I thought perhaps that was the reason he went upriver.'

'He was only restless. He doesn't take to trap life, and

right now he doesn't have to stay on it all day. Do you think it bothered Mom?'

'No,' she said slowly. 'We didn't talk about it. We were too busy talking about other things.'

Then she thought this was really what Rod and Jeff and she had been trying to do yesterday afternoon when she'd spent so long telling them about the Orient and Jeff had kept asking questions. Talking about everything except salmon was the only way she could help now.

It went on like this, day after day, with tension growing, and both trying hard not to show it. There were tender moments too, when she realized how much it meant to Rod to have her share the waiting. Now, since she had told him about the failure of the Lady Luck and why her father had listened only to Mr Daniels' version, he understood some of the things she'd only hinted at before.

'I didn't know how hard it had been for you, Judy. You've been wonderful about it. But will your father feel any different when Daniels is only too glad to buy our fish?'

'Of course! He'll be the first to admit how wrong he was. He'll be thrilled about the river! I know that, Rod.'

As the days passed, they spoke less and less about the river. She tried to fill the hours with small talk about things that seemed of no consequence to either of them—gossip of the mine, members of the crew, the new guest house she and Alec were planning, anything at all. At last Judy thought she could bear it no longer. They'd been over to visit Jeff on his trap, and he'd been unusually silent. So was Rod, she thought, as they sat in the cabin of the *Working Stiff*. He must be thinking, as she was, that it was now nine days since the fifteenth.

'Why haven't the pinks come, Rod?' she asked suddenly. 'Do you know any reason why they shouldn't?'

'It could be anything,' he said. 'A storm at sea, heavy winds, big currents to hold them back or even force them on another route. All I know is what Spence tells us. Daniels is getting his fish from far up the coast, and Jim Matson is sending his purse seiners up there. But what it means, Judy, I couldn't—' He leaped to his feet and paced the cabin. 'I've tried to think what it meant. Do you think I haven't worried this last week?

'But I do know this.' He stopped before her. 'I know that last year and the year before there was a run of pinks on this river. I've got the count of spawners. And I know those eggs weren't washed out by spring freshets. There weren't any big floods those two springs. I know! I kept watch on this river. Those fingerlings went out to sea. And they'll be back. They're bound to come, Judy! That's the only way I can see it.'

She put out her hand, feeling the need to touch him. He sat down and drew her close. Never had she been more conscious of a strength and surety about him. It wasn't that her own faith had faltered, but she needed to hear him tell her his hadn't.

'I'm so glad I came today,' she said.

'And you're coming tomorrow?'

'I can't, Rod! I promised Alec we'd decide about the new guest house and make the list of everthing we needed so Carl could buy it on the *Betsy*'s trip to Juneau. And if the pink run should come, and I didn't know it, I couldn't bear it!'

'You'll be the first to know. I'll stop at Shaman Cove on my way to Rampart to see Daniels. So when you hear me blow the whistle you'll know—'

'Promise? Surely?'

'Who would I rather tell than you, Judy?' he asked as he kissed her. 'I've thought about that moment almost more than the coming of the pinks.' His voice was husky. 'Without you, Judy, this river wouldn't mean so much to me—not any more.'

All morning as Judy worked on the plans for the guest house and wrote out the shopping list, she listened for the whistle of Rod's boat. It seemed that at any moment she must hear the familiar signal. When the *Betsy* finally departed for Juneau in early afternoon, she was tempted to go to Tallac Bay, then thought it was so late she couldn't have a real visit. Rod wasn't expecting her, so he wouldn't be disappointed.

Next day she wished desperately she had gone when she wakened to find a black curtain of rain falling. Clouds hung low over the water, and the strait wore a sullen air of threat.

'Something bad's coming out of this,' Alec said. 'Even now it's so thick you'd be lost before you'd gone half a mile.'

'But won't it clear?'

'Don't know, Judy. I don't like the way it looks. And the *Betsy*'s up in Juneau.'

The next morning waves were breaking on the strait and the barometer was falling.

'Might be in for a south-easter,' Alec said.

Her heart sank. 'That might last for days,' she said slowly.

He nodded. 'Can tell better by night. Hope Carl got started back early. He's got some heavy machinery on that afterdeck.'

Judy heard the *Betsy* pull in long after dark. A few hours later the south-easter struck. For three days the strait was a white smother of rain and spume. Judy doubted if Rod could get to Rampart if the pinks had come, but as she watched with the glasses, she saw an occasional craft pitching and rolling to fight its way against the gale funnelling through the three-hundred-mile slit between the mountains.

At noon, on the fourth day of the south-easter, the wind switched and blew even harder from the south-west. Judy's thoughts were despairing. It had been seven days since she'd seen Rod. But Alec was smiling when he came to supper.

'Had to blow itself out sometime, Judy. Though often it doesn't appear it's ever going to.'

Even now Judy couldn't believe it would as she listened to the gale howling around the cook camp. For days, although she had tried to mask her tension with an appearance of outward calm, she knew she had been edgy with frayed nerves. She'd seen her father looking at her strangely. He had been more than scrupulous in keeping his promise not to speak about Tallac River until the outcome was a certainty, but she knew it was in his thoughts during the odd silences that fell between them.

Next morning the sea was gleaming in bright sunshine. The air was clear and rain-washed. Alec only nodded when she told him she was going across the strait. As she was leaving, her father came out of his office.

'How about running me up to Rampart Bay, Judy?' he asked. 'I have to get off a cable.'

'Today!' She was startled by the vehemence in her voice. 'Why can't the *Betsy* take you?'

'Judy,' he said. 'Don't you see how useless it is to go on hoping? For days I've watched you and wished we could talk about this. I've waited, as I'd promised, over two weeks after you thought the fish would come. And now, if you go over to Tallac, you'll only be more stirred up about this. By this time even Rod must admit there'll be no salmon in that river.'

'And if he does— If something has happened—something no one could be expected to know— If the pinks haven't come, and he doesn't believe they will, I want to— I'm going to be with him!'

She ran out of the house and to the float.

As she crossed the glassy strait, her spirits began to soar. In less than two hours she would be with Rod. Perhaps the delay wasn't the threat she had imagined. It had been not knowing what it meant or what had happened that had been so frightening, but now soon that would be over. By the time she reached the harbour she only wondered that any doubts had ever come to her. And this was the way she wanted to feel when she saw Rod.

He made her boat fast, and she stepped out on the little platform.

'They didn't come, Judy.' His voice was empty. 'Tomorrow I was going over to tell you.'

'But they will! It's too soon to give up, Rod!'

'More than two weeks? With the purse seiners making hauls? No, Judy. I might as well admit it. But if I only knew what happened! I've gone over everything! I was so sure! And I had a right to be!'

'Does Jeff think they won't come?'

'He doesn't say it, but he must know. He's only trying to make me feel better about what I've done to them. As though I hadn't thought about it! Spence's savings for another boat. Jeff's timber and all his work. Even the money in his coffee can. And for what! A couple of useless traps we couldn't sell even if we tried!'

'It was more than traps, Rod. It was something they will always have.'

'What?'

'A belief in you. Just as I have. Whether the salmon come or not.'

He turned and strode away, caulks biting deep into the long timber of the trap. She knew at that moment he couldn't have spoken, but she'd had to tell him how she felt. She watched him lean over, pull up the cotton webbing to clean it. At any other time he wouldn't have noticed the small bits of seaweed, but now he picked them off, one by one, as he fought off despair. After a long time he straightened up and stood there at the other end of the trap looking out at the mouth of the bay. Suddenly she saw his body stiffen.

'Judy!' he yelled. 'They're finning!' He ran toward her. 'Look, Judy! They're finning!'

She looked. The water's surface near the entrance seemed to be boiling. A fish jumped, then another, and another.

'They've come!' she cried. 'I knew it! Oh, I knew it!'

He was beside her now.

'Jeff! Jeff!' he yelled. 'The pinks! Look at them come!'

Jeff erupted from his shack, stared a moment, then waved his hat. The three stood cheering. Judy was laughing and crying as she and Rod stood with their arms around each other.

'Look, Judy, they're coming along the shore headed for the lead!'

'And the whole bay is full of fish!' she cried.

'They had to come! They had to come!' It was a chant of victory.

Rod untied her boat. 'Get in,' he said, and shoved the

craft along the log to the pot in the centre. 'They're following the lead. Be in the hearts soon. Watch the tunnel to see the first salmon to come into a Baird trap!'

Judy stared at the empty water. It was so clear she could see the webbing far down. She looked farther, and beneath the heavy timber on the other side, in the hearts of the traps, the water was suddenly solid with the bodies of gleaming fish.

'Rod! Hundreds of them!'

'Hundreds! Thousands! The traps'll fill up in a hurry. I've got to get to Rampart and see Daniels.' He started for his motor boat.

'The *Working Stiff* is faster. Jump aboard.' She went below and started the motor. 'I'm going to be with you when you see Mr Daniels.'

He took the wheel and turned toward the other trap. 'Got to tell Jeff,' he said.

As they approached, Jeff was staring into the water at the lead. The fish had just reached him.

'Look at 'em pouring in!' he shouted. 'What'd I tell you just this morning!'

'You and Judy!' Rod said. 'We're going to Rampart, and if the spillers fill up before the cannery tender gets here, you'll have to close the traps.'

'Close 'em? Not on your life! Tell Daniels to get here in a hurry.'

The *Working Stiff* ran full throttle out of the bay. Rod was at the wheel. Judy stood beside him, her arm around him. The sparkling strait was a shimmering path before them. For a long time they didn't speak. They didn't need words.

It was a voyage of pure enchantment.

———————

For other books by Kathrene Pinkerton, please see next page

If you have enjoyed reading *The Secret River*,
you will want to know more about the Baird family.
Kathrene Pinkerton's first book about them is

Hidden Harbour

which takes up their story not long after they had arrived in
Alaska. Jeff Baird was content with the wealth of game and
fish and the great stands of timber that the country had to
offer. Mary Baird, his wife, had to bring up the children in
an empty and lonely land, with only her husband's earnings
from hand-logging on which to live. And of the children,
Spence was competent and understanding, but Vicky and
Rob, already in their teens, were longing for closer contact
with the outside world.

The trouble began when Spence discovered that there
was dry rot—bad dry rot—in the hull of the family sloop,
their only means of contact with civilization. The story that
follows is often tensely exciting, and always full of interest.

The sequel to *Hidden Harbour* is

Second Meeting

which is mainly Vicky Baird's story. Vicky is now eighteen, and her longing to see a bit more of the outside world increases with every year. By a stroke of luck, she is invited to become one of the guests on board a luxurious yacht cruising round the Alaskan coast, and it is here that she meets, for the second time, a young artist called Philip Trent. And, as readers of *The Secret River* know, Vicky is soon to lose her heart to Phil.

In *Second Meeting* we again meet all the Baird family, Jeff, Mary, Spence, Rod, and of course Vicky, and after only the first few pages of this delightful story, we are sharing their joys and troubles, their disappointments and successes.

There are two other books
by Kathrene Pinkerton that you will enjoy

Partners in the Wilds

is the story of how fifteen-year-old Neal Bartlett joins forces
with old Tom Clark in the exciting business of mink breeding. Tom has been mink trapping and breeding for years,
and when Neal puts forward his latest scientific ideas, there
are clashes of opinion. The author tells of the growth of
understanding between the partners; they have a common
belief that what they are doing is important, and their
relationship becomes closer through their many set backs.

[SEE OVER]

Royal Browne

is about seventeen-year-old Royal and her younger brother, Wally. Their father, Captain Danforth Browne, had given up his profession as an actor when he had inherited a small legacy, and with the money he bought an old yacht, the *Argosy*, which he converted into a sea-going store. Visiting the loggers and their families on the wild and rocky coast of British Columbia was just the life for Wally, who never doubted that his future lay in this fast-growing land, but it was hard for Royal to decide, especially after they encounter a showboat with its gay crew of actors.